Sir Gawain and the Green Knight, The Lady of Shallot, The Lady of the Fountain, and other Classic Poems and Tales of Camelot

Sir Gawain and the Green Knight, The Lady of Shallot, The Lady of the Fountain, and other Classic Poems and Tales of Camelot

Published: March 2011 (Paperback and Kindle)

Limitless Press LLC
Jupiter, FL

ISBN 13 Digits: 978-1-61335-003-4 (Paperback)
　　　　　　　　978-1-61335-004-1 (Kindle)

Library of Congress Control Number: 2011923810

http://www.limitlesspress.com
publisher@limitlesspress.com

All rights reserved.

The works reproduced in this book are understood to be in the public domain and no longer subject to copyright laws. No copyright is sought or claimed on these works. Original text was compiled from free sources with no claim of copyright. Very little editing was done to the original text other than to format it for the printed page.

Cover art is *God Speed!* (1900) by Edmund Leighton.

Back cover art is *The Lady of Shallot* (1888) by John William Waterhouse.

Cover art for this book is subject to copyright by the publisher:

Limitless Press LLC, March 2011

Short Biographies of the Authors

Alfred Tennyson, 1st Baron (Lord) Tennyson (1809-1892) was Poet Laureate of the United Kingdom during much of Queen Victoria's reign and remains one of the most popular poets in the English language. Tennyson excelled at penning short lyrics. Much of his verse was based on classical mythological themes. *The Lady of Shallot* was published in his second book of poetry in 1833.

Jessie L Weston (1850-1928) was an independent scholar and folklorist, working mainly on mediaeval Arthurian texts. She received acclaim for her translation of *Sir Gawain and the Green Knight* in 1898. In addition to her translations of poems from Old into Modern English, her best-known work is *From Ritual to Romance* published in 1920.

Layamon was a poet of the early 13th century and author of the Brut, a notable English poem of the 12th century that was the first English language work to discuss the legends of Arthur and the Knights of the Round Table. His poem provided inspiration for numerous later writers, including Sir Thomas Malory and Jorge Luis Borges, and had an impact on medieval history writing in England.

Lady Charlotte Elizabeth Guest (1812-1895) was an English businesswoman and translator. An important figure in the study of Welsh literature and the Welsh language, she is best known for her pioneering English translation of the major medieval work, the *Mabinogion*. *The Lady of the Fountain* is a key piece of that epic work.

Wilfrid Scawen Blunt (1840-1922) was an English poet and writer. He is best known for his poetry, which was published in a collected edition in 1914, but also wrote a number of political essays and polemics. In addition to his poetry, he was a well known explorer who travelled through Spain, Algeria, Egypt, the Syrian Desert, and extensively in the Middle East and India.

Rachel Annand Taylor (1876-1960) was a Scottish poet, biographer and literary critic. She was one of the first women to study at Aberdeen University. She later taught at Aberdeen High School for Girls. As a writer she was admired by Richard Aldington, G.K. Chesterton, Hilaire Belloc and D. H. Lawrence. In 1943 she was awarded an honorary LLD from Aberdeen University.

William Morris (1834-1896) was an English textile designer, artist, and writer. Morris wrote and published poetry, fiction, and translations of ancient and medieval texts throughout his life. *Sir Galahad, a Christmas Mystery* was published in 1858 in the collection called *The Defense of Guinevere and Other Poems*.

Contents

Sir Gawain and the Green Knight	pg. 1
The Lady of Shallot	pg. 44
The Founding of the Round Table	pg. 47
The Passing of Arthur	pg. 51
The Morte D'arthur	pg. 61
The Lady of the Fountain	pg. 62
Arthurian Songs: 1. Avalon	pg. 83
Sir Galahad, a Christmas Mystery	pg. 84

Sir Gawain and the Green Knight, The Lady of Shallot, The Lady of the Fountain, and other Classic Poems and Tales of Camelot

Sir Gawain and the Green Knight
Translated by Jessie L. Weston (1898)

Preface to First Edition

The poem of which the following pages offer a prose rendering is contained in a MS., believed to be unique, of the Cottonian Collection, Nero A.X., preserved in the British Museum. The MS. is of the end of the fourteenth century, but it is possible that the composition of the poem is somewhat earlier; the subject-matter is certainly of very old date. There has been a considerable divergence of opinion among scholars on the question of authorship, but the view now generally accepted is that it is the work of the same hand as Pearl, another poem of considerable merit contained in the same MS.

Our poem, or, to speak more correctly, metrical romance, contains over 2500 lines, and is composed in staves of varying length, ending in five short rhyming lines, technically known as a bob and a wheel,--the lines forming the body of the stave being not rhyming, but alliterative. The dialect in which it is written has been decided to be West Midland, probably Lancashire, and is by no means easy to understand. Indeed, it is the real difficulty and obscurity of the language, which, in spite of careful and scholarly editing, will always place the poem in its original form outside the range of any but professed students of mediæval literature, which has encouraged me to make an attempt to render it more accessible to the general public, by giving it a form that shall be easily intelligible, and at the same time preserve as closely as possible the style of the author.

For that style, in spite of a certain roughness, unavoidable at a period in which the language was still in a partially developed and amorphous stage, is really charming. The author has a keen eye for effect; a talent for description, detailed without becoming wearisome; a genuine love of Nature and sympathy with her varying moods; and a real refinement and elevation of feeling which enable him to deal with a risqué: situation with an absence of coarseness, not, unfortunately, to be always met with in a mediæval writer. Standards of taste vary with the age, but even judged by that of our own day the author of Sir Gawain and the Green Knight comes not all too badly out of the ordeal!

The story with which the poem deals, too, has claims upon our interest. I have shown elsewhere (1) that the beheading challenge is an incident of very early occurrence in heroic legend, and that the particular form given to it in the English poem is especially interesting, corresponding as it does to the variations of the story as preserved in the oldest known version, that of the old Irish Fled Bricrend.

But in no other version is the incident coupled with that of a temptation and testing of the hero's honour and chastity, such as meets us here. At first sight one is inclined to assign the episode of the lady of the castle to the class of stories of which the oldest version is preserved in Biblical record--the story of Joseph and Potiphar's wife; a motif not unseldom employed by mediæval writers, and which notably occurs in what we may call the Launfal group of stories. But there are certain points which may make us hesitate as to whether in its first conception the tale was really one of this class.

It must be noted that here the lady is acting throughout with the knowledge and consent of the husband, an important point of difference. In the second place, it is very doubtful whether her entire attitude was not a ruse. From the Green Knight's words to Gawain when he finally reveals himself, "I wot we shall soon make peace with my wife, who was thy bitter enemy," her conduct hardly seems to have been prompted by real passion.

In my Studies on the Legend of Sir Gawain, already referred to, I have suggested that the character of the lady here is, perhaps, a reminiscence of that of the Queen of the Magic Castle or Isle, daughter or niece of an enchanter, who at an early stage of Gawain's story was undoubtedly his love. I think it not impossible that she was an integral part of the tale as first told, and her rôle here was determined by that which she originally played. In most versions of the story she has dropped out altogether. It is, of course, possible that, there being but a confused reminiscence of the original tale, her share may have been modified by the influence of the Launfal group; but I should prefer to explain the episode on the whole as a somewhat distorted survival of an original feature.

But in any case we may be thankful for this, that the author of the most important English metrical romance dealing with Arthurian legend faithfully adheres to the original conception of Gawain's character, as drawn before the monkish lovers of edification laid their ruthless hands on his legend, and turned the model of knightly virtues and courtesy into a mere vulgar libertine.

Brave, chivalrous, loyally faithful to his plighted word, scrupulously heedful of his own and others' honour, Gawain stands before us in this poem. We take up Malory or Tennyson, and in spite of their charm of style, in spite of the halo of religious mysticism in which they have striven to enwrap their characters, we lay them down with a feeling of dissatisfaction. How did the Gawain of their imagination, this empty-headed, empty-hearted worldling, cruel murderer, and treacherous friend, ever come to be the typical English hero? For such Gawain certainly was, even more than Arthur himself. Then we turn back to these faded pages, and read the quaintly earnest words in which the old writer reveals the hidden meaning of that mystic symbol, the pentangle, and vindicates Gawain's title to claim it as his badge--and we smile, perhaps, but we cease to wonder at the widespread popularity of King Arthur's famous nephew, or at the immense body of romance that claims him as its hero.

Scholars know all this, of course; they can read the poem for themselves in its original rough and intricate phraseology; perhaps they will be shocked at an attempt to handle it in simpler form. But this little book is not for them, and if to those to whom the tale would otherwise be a sealed treasure these pages bring some new knowledge of the way in which our forefathers looked on the characters of the Arthurian legend, the tales they told of them (unconsciously betraying the while how they themselves lived and thought and spoke)--if by that means they gain a keener appreciation of our national heroes, a wider knowledge of our national literature,--then the spirit of the long-dead poet will doubtless not be the slowest to pardon my handling of what was his masterpiece, as it is, in M. Gaston Paris' words, "The jewel of English mediæval literature."

BOURNEMOUTH, June 1898

Preface to Second Edition

In preparing this Second Edition I have adopted certain suggestions of the late Professor Kölbing, contained in a review published by him in Englische Studien xxvi. In one or two instances, however, I have not felt free to follow his reading--e.g., in þrynne syþe must certainly mean "for the third time," not "thrice." The lady has already kissed Gawain twice during the interview; Professor Kölbing's suggestion would make him receive five kisses, instead of three, the correct number. Nor do I think the story would gain anything by reproducing the details of the dissection of animals. This little series is not intended for scholars, who can study the original works for themselves, but for the general public, and I have therefore avoided any digression from the main thread of the story. In the main, however, I have gladly availed myself of the late Professor's learned criticisms.

BOURNEMOUTH, May 1900

Sir Gawain and the Green Knight

After the siege and the assault of Troy, when that burg was destroyed and burnt to ashes, and the traitor tried for his treason, the noble Æneas and his kin sailed forth to become princes and patrons of well-nigh all the Western Isles. Thus Romulus built Rome (and gave to the city his own name, which it bears even to this day); and Ticius turned him to Tuscany; and Langobard raised him up dwellings in Lombardy; and Felix Brutus sailed far over the French flood, and founded the kingdom of Britain, wherein have been war and waste and wonder, and bliss and bale, ofttimes since.

And in that kingdom of Britain have been wrought more gallant deeds than in any other; but of all British kings Arthur was the most valiant, as I have heard tell, therefore will I set forth a wondrous adventure that fell out in his time. And if ye will listen to me, but for a little while, I will tell it even as it stands in story stiff and strong, fixed in the letter, as it hath long been known in the land.

King Arthur lay at Camelot upon a Christmas-tide, with many a gallant lord and lovely lady, and all the noble brotherhood of the Round Table. There they held rich revels with gay talk and jest; one while they would ride forth to joust and tourney, and again back to the court to make carols; (2) for there was the feast holden fifteen days with all the mirth that men could devise, song and glee, glorious to hear, in the daytime, and dancing at night. Halls and chambers were crowded with noble guests, the bravest of knights and the loveliest of ladies, and Arthur himself was the comeliest king that ever held a court. For all this fair folk were in their youth, the fairest and most fortunate under heaven, and the king himself of such fame that it were hard now to name so valiant a hero.

Now the New Year had but newly come in, and on that day a double portion was served on the high table to all the noble guests, and thither came the king with all his knights, when the service in the chapel had been sung to an end. And they greeted each other for the New Year, and gave rich gifts, the one to the other (and they that received them were not wroth, that may ye well believe!), and the maidens laughed and made mirth till it was time to get them to meat. Then they washed and sat them down to the feast in fitting rank and order, and Guinevere the queen, gaily clad, sat on the high daïs. Silken was her seat, with a fair canopy over her head, of rich tapestries of Tars, embroidered, and studded with costly gems; fair she was to look upon, with her shining grey eyes, a fairer woman might no man boast himself of having seen.

But Arthur would not eat till all were served, so full of joy and gladness was he, even as a child; he liked not either to lie long, or to sit long at meat, so worked upon him his young blood and his wild brain. And another custom he had also, that came of his nobility, that he would never eat upon an high day till he had been advised of some knightly deed, or some strange and marvellous tale, of his ancestors, or of arms, or of other ventures. Or till some stranger knight should seek of him leave to joust with one of the Round Table, that they might set their lives in jeopardy, one against another, as fortune might favour them. Such was the king's custom when he sat in hall at each high feast with his noble knights, therefore on that New Year tide, he abode, fair of face, on the throne, and made much mirth withal.

Thus the king sat before the high tables, and spake of many things; and there good Sir Gawain was seated by Guinevere the queen, and on her other side sat Agravain, à la dure main; (3) both were the king's sister's sons and full gallant knights. And at the end of the table was Bishop Bawdewyn, and Ywain, King Urien's son, sat at the other side alone. These were worthily served on the daïs, and at the lower tables sat many valiant knights. Then they bare the first course with the blast of trumpets and waving of banners, with the sound of drums and pipes, of song and lute, that many a heart was uplifted at the melody. Many were the dainties, and rare the meats, so great was the plenty they might scarce find room on the board to set on the dishes. Each helped himself as he liked best, and to each two were twelve dishes, with great plenty of beer and wine.

Now I will say no more of the service, but that ye may know there was no lack, for there drew near a venture that the folk might well have left their labour to gaze upon. As the sound of the music ceased, and the first course had been fitly served, there came in at the hall door one terrible to behold, of stature greater than any on earth; from neck to loin so strong and thickly made, and with limbs so long and so great that he seemed even as a giant. And yet he was but a man, only the mightiest that might mount a steed; broad of chest and shoulders and slender of waist, and all his features of like fashion; but men marvelled much at his colour, for he rode even as a knight, yet was green all over.

For he was clad all in green, with a straight coat, and a mantle above; all decked and lined with fur was the cloth and the hood that was thrown back from his locks and lay on his shoulders. Hose had he of the same green, and spurs of bright gold with silken fastenings richly worked; and all his vesture was verily green. Around his waist and his saddle were bands with fair stones set upon silken work, 'twere too long to tell of all the trifles that were embroidered thereon--birds and insects in gay gauds of green and gold. All the trappings of his steed were of metal of like enamel, even the stirrups that he stood in stained of the same, and stirrups and saddle-bow alike gleamed and shone with green stones. Even the steed on which he rode was of the same hue, a green horse, great and strong, and hard to hold, with broidered bridle, meet for the rider.

The knight was thus gaily dressed in green, his hair falling around his shoulders; on his breast hung a beard, as thick and green as a bush, and the beard and the hair of his head were clipped all round above his elbows. The lower part of his sleeves were fastened with clasps in the same wise as a king's mantle. The horse's mane was crisp and plaited with many a knot folded in with gold thread about the fair green, here a twist of the hair, here another of gold. The tail was twined in like manner, and both were bound about with a band of bright green set with many a precious stone; then they were tied aloft in a cunning knot, whereon rang many bells of burnished gold. Such a steed might no other ride, nor had such ever been looked upon in that hall ere that time; and all who saw that knight spake and said that a man might scarce abide his stroke.

The knight bore no helm nor hauberk, neither gorget nor breast-plate, neither shaft nor buckler to smite nor to shield, but in one hand he had a holly-bough, that is greenest when the groves are bare, and in his other an axe, huge and uncomely, a cruel weapon in fashion, if one would picture it. The head was an ell-yard long, the metal all of green steel and gold, the blade burnished bright, with a broad edge, as well shapen to shear as a sharp razor. The steel was set into a strong staff, all bound round with iron, even to the end, and engraved with green in cunning work. A lace was twined about it, that looped at the head, and all adown the handle it was clasped with tassels on buttons of bright green richly broidered.

The knight rideth through the entrance of the hall, driving straight to the high daïs, and greeted no man, but looked ever upwards; and the first words he spake were, "Where is the ruler of this folk? I would gladly look upon that hero, and have speech with him." He cast his eyes on the knights, and mustered them up and down, striving ever to see who of them was of most renown.

Then was there great gazing to behold that chief, for each man marvelled what it might mean that a knight and his steed should have even such a hue as the green grass; and that seemed even greener than green enamel on bright gold. All looked on him as he stood, and drew near unto him wondering greatly what he might be; for many marvels had they seen, but none such as this, and phantasm and faërie did the folk deem it. Therefore were the gallant knights slow to answer, and gazed astounded, and sat stone still in a deep silence through that goodly hall, as if a slumber were fallen upon them. I deem it was not all for doubt, but some for courtesy that they might give ear unto his errand.

Then Arthur beheld this adventurer before his high daïs, and knightly he greeted him, for fearful was he never. "Sir," he said, "thou art welcome to this place--lord of this hall am I, and men call me Arthur. Light thee down, and tarry awhile, and what thy will is, that shall we learn after."

"Nay," quoth the stranger, "so help me He that sitteth on high, 'twas not mine errand to tarry any while in this dwelling; but the praise of this thy folk and thy city is lifted up on high, and thy warriors are holden for the best and the most valiant of those who ride mail-clad to the fight. The wisest and the worthiest of this world are they, and well proven in all knightly sports. And here, as I have heard tell, is fairest courtesy, therefore have I come hither as at this time. Ye may be sure by the branch that I bear here that I come in peace, seeking no strife. For had I willed to journey in warlike guise I have at home both hauberk and helm, shield and shining spear, and other weapons to mine hand, but since I seek no war my raiment is that of peace. But if thou be as bold as all men tell thou wilt freely grant me the boon I ask."

And Arthur answered, "Sir Knight, if thou cravest battle here thou shalt not fail for lack of a foe."

And the knight answered, "Nay, I ask no fight, in faith here on the benches are but beardless children, were I clad in armour on my steed there is no man here might match me. Therefore I ask in this court but a Christmas jest, for that it is Yule-tide, and New Year, and there are here many fain for sport. If any one in this hall holds himself so hardy, (4) so bold both of blood and brain, as to dare strike me one stroke for another, I will give him as a gift this axe, which is heavy enough, in sooth, to handle as he may list, and I will abide the first blow, unarmed as I sit. If any knight be so bold as to prove my words let him come swiftly to me here, and take this weapon, I quit claim to it, he may keep it as his own, and I will abide his stroke, firm on the floor. Then shalt thou give me the right to deal him another, the respite of a year and a day shall he have. Now haste, and let see whether any here dare say aught."

Now if the knights had been astounded at the first, yet stiller were they all, high and low, when they had heard his words. The knight on his steed straightened himself in the saddle, and rolled his eyes fiercely round the hall, red they gleamed under his green and bushy brows. He frowned and twisted his beard, waiting to see who should rise, and when none answered he cried aloud in mockery, "What, is this Arthur's hall, and these the knights whose renown hath run through many realms? Where are now your pride and your conquests, your wrath, and anger, and mighty words? Now are the praise and the renown of the Round Table overthrown by one man's speech, since all keep silence for dread ere ever they have seen a blow!"

With that he laughed so loudly that the blood rushed to the king's fair face for very shame; he waxed wroth, as did all his knights, and sprang to his feet, and drew near to the stranger and said, "Now by heaven foolish is thy asking, and thy folly shall find its fitting answer. I know no man aghast at thy great words. Give me here thine axe and I shall grant thee the boon thou hast asked." Lightly he sprang to him and caught at his hand, and the knight, fierce of aspect, lighted down from his charger.

Then Arthur took the axe and gripped the haft, and swung it round, ready to strike. And the knight stood before him, taller by the head than any in the hall; he stood, and stroked his beard, and drew down his coat, no more dismayed for the king's threats than if one had brought him a drink of wine.

Then Gawain, who sat by the queen, leaned forward to the king and spake, "I beseech ye, my lord, let this venture be mine. Would ye but bid me rise from this seat, and stand by your side, so that my liege lady thought it not ill, then would I come to your counsel before this goodly court. For I think it not seemly when such challenges be made in your hall that ye yourself should undertake it, while there are many bold knights who sit beside ye, none are there, methinks, of readier will under heaven, or more valiant in open field. I am the weakest, I wot, and the feeblest of wit, and it will be the less loss of my life if ye seek sooth. For save that ye are mine uncle naught is there in me to praise, no virtue is there in my body save your blood, and since this challenge is such folly that it beseems ye not to take it, and I have asked it from ye first, let it fall to me, and if I bear myself ungallantly then let all this court blame me."

Then they all spake with one voice that the king should leave this venture and grant it to Gawain.

Then Arthur commanded the knight to rise, and he rose up quickly and knelt down before the king, and caught hold of the weapon; and the king loosed his hold of it, and lifted up his hand, and gave him his blessing, and bade him be strong both of heart and hand. "Keep thee well, nephew," quoth Arthur, "that thou give him but the one blow, and if thou redest him rightly I trow thou shalt well abide the stroke he may give thee after."

Gawain stepped to the stranger, axe in hand, and he, never fearing, awaited his coming. Then the Green Knight spake to Sir Gawain, "Make we our covenant ere we go further. First, I ask thee, knight, what is thy name? Tell me truly, that I may know thee."

"In faith," quoth the good knight, "Gawain am I, who give thee this buffet, let what may come of it; and at this time twelvemonth will I take another at thine hand with whatsoever weapon thou wilt, and none other."

Then the other answered again, "Sir Gawain, so may I thrive as I am fain to take this buffet at thine hand," and he quoth further, "Sir Gawain, it liketh me well that I shall take at thy fist that which I have asked here, and thou hast readily and truly rehearsed all the covenant that I asked of the king, save that thou shalt swear me, by thy troth, to seek me thyself wherever thou hopest that I may be found, and win thee such reward as thou dealest me to-day, before this folk."

"Where shall I seek thee?" quoth Gawain. "Where is thy place? By Him that made me, I wot never where thou dwellest, nor know I thee, knight, thy court, nor thy name. But teach me truly all that pertaineth thereto, and tell me thy name, and I shall use all my wit to win my way thither, and that I swear thee for sooth, and by my sure troth."

"That is enough in the New Year, it needs no more," quoth the Green Knight to the gallant Gawain, "if I tell thee truly when I have taken the blow, and thou hast smitten me; then will I teach thee of my house and home, and mine own name, then mayest thou ask thy road and keep covenant. And if I waste no words then farest thou the better, for thou canst dwell in thy land, and seek no further. But take now thy toll, and let see how thy strikest."

"Gladly will I," quoth Gawain, handling his axe.

Then the Green Knight swiftly made him ready, he bowed down his head, and laid his long locks on the crown that his bare neck might be seen. Gawain gripped his axe and raised it on high, the left foot he set forward on the floor, and let the blow fall lightly on the bare neck. The sharp edge of the blade sundered the bones, smote through the neck, and clave it in two, so that the edge of the steel bit on the ground, and the fair head fell to the earth that many struck it with their feet as it rolled forth. The blood spurted forth, and glistened on the green raiment, but the knight neither faltered nor fell; he started forward with out-stretched hand, and caught the head, and lifted it up; then he turned to his steed, and took hold of the bride, set his foot in the stirrup, and mounted. His head he held by the hair, in his hand. Then he seated himself in his saddle as if naught ailed him, and he were not headless. He turned his steed about, the grim corpse bleeding freely the while, and they who looked upon him doubted them much for the covenant.

For he held up the head in his hand, and turned the face towards them that sat on the high daïs, and it lifted up the eyelids and looked upon them and spake as ye shall hear. "Look, Gawain, that thou art ready to go as thou hast promised, and seek leally till thou find me, even as thou hast sworn in this hall in the hearing of these knights. Come thou, I charge thee, to the Green Chapel, such a stroke as thou hast dealt thou hast deserved, and it shall be promptly paid thee on New Year's morn. Many men know me as the knight of the Green Chapel, and if thou askest, thou shalt not fail to find me. Therefore it behoves thee to come, or to yield thee as recreant."

With that he turned his bridle, and galloped out at the hall door, his head in his hands, so that the sparks flew from beneath his horse's hoofs. Whither he went none knew, no more than they wist whence he had come; and the king and Gawain they gazed and laughed, for in sooth this had proved a greater marvel than any they had known aforetime.

Though Arthur the king was astonished at his heart, yet he let no sign of it be seen, but spake in courteous wise to the fair queen: "Dear lady, be not dismayed, such craft is well suited to Christmas-tide when we seek jesting, laughter and song, and fair carols of knights and ladies. But now I may well get me to meat, for I have seen a marvel I may not forget." Then he looked on Sir Gawain, and said gaily, "Now, fair nephew, hang up thine axe, since it has hewn enough," and they hung it on the dossal above the daïs, where all men might look on it for a marvel, and by its true token tell of the wonder. Then the twain sat them down together, the king and the good knight, and men served them with a double portion, as was the share of the noblest, with all manner of meat and of minstrelsy. And they spent that day in gladness, but Sir Gawain must well bethink him of the heavy venture to which he had set his hand.

This beginning of adventures had Arthur at the New Year; for he yearned to hear gallant tales, though his words were few when he sat at the feast. But now had they stern work on hand. Gawain was glad to begin the jest in the hall, but ye need have no marvel if the end be heavy. For though a man be merry in mind when he has well drunk, yet a year runs full swiftly, and the beginning but rarely matches the end.

For Yule was now over-past, (5) and the year after, each season in its turn following the other. For after Christmas comes crabbed Lent, that will have fish for flesh and simpler cheer. But then the weather of the world chides with winter; the cold withdraws itself, the clouds uplift, and the rain falls in warm showers on the fair plains. Then the flowers come forth, meadows and grove are clad in green, the birds make ready to build, and sing sweetly for solace of the soft summer that follows thereafter. The blossoms bud and blow in the hedgerows rich and rank, and noble notes enough are heard in the fair woods.

After the season of summer, with the soft winds, when zephyr breathes lightly on seeds and herbs, joyous indeed is the growth that waxes thereout when the dew drips from the leaves beneath the blissful glance of the bright sun. But then comes harvest and hardens the grain, warning it to wax ripe ere the winter. The drought drives the dust on high, flying over the face of the land; the angry wind of the welkin wrestles with the sun; the leaves fall from the trees and light upon the ground, and all brown are the groves that but now were green, and ripe is the fruit that once was flower. So the year passes into many yesterdays, and winter comes again, as it needs no sage to tell us.

When the Michaelmas moon was come in with warnings of winter, Sir Gawain bethought him full oft of his perilous journey. Yet till All Hallows Day he lingered with Arthur, and on that day they made a great feast for the hero's sake, with much revel and richness of the Round Table. Courteous knights and comely ladies, all were in sorrow for the love of that knight, and though they spake no word of it, many were joyless for his sake.

And after meat, sadly Sir Gawain turned to his uncle, and spake of his journey, and said, "Liege lord of my life, leave from you I crave. Ye know well how the matter stands without more words, to-morrow am I bound to set forth in search of the Green Knight."

Then came together all the noblest knights, Ywain and Erec, and many another. Sir Dodinel le Sauvage, the Duke of Clarence, Launcelot and Lionel, and Lucan the Good, Sir Bors and Sir Bedivere, valiant knights both, and many another hero, with Sir Mador de la Porte, and they all drew near, heavy at heart, to take counsel with Sir Gawain. Much sorrow and weeping was there in the hall to think that so worthy a knight as Gawain should wend his way to seek a deadly blow, and should no more wield his sword in fight. But the knight made ever good cheer, and said, "Nay, wherefore should I shrink? What may a man do but prove his fate?"

He dwelt there all that day, and on the morn he arose and asked betimes for his armour; and they brought it unto him on this wise: first, a rich carpet was stretched on the floor (6) (and brightly did the gold gear glitter upon it), then the knight stepped on to it, and handled the steel; clad he was in a doublet of silk, with a close hood, lined fairly throughout. Then they set the steel shoes upon his feet, and wrapped his legs with greaves, with polished knee-caps, fastened with knots of gold. Then they cased his thighs in cuisses closed with thongs, and brought him the byrny of bright steel rings sewn upon a fair stuff. Well burnished braces they set on each arm with good elbow-pieces, and gloves of mail, and all the goodly gear that should shield him in his need. And they cast over all a rich surcoat, and set the golden spurs on his heels, and girt him with a trusty sword fastened with a silken bawdrick. When he was thus clad his harness was costly, for the least loop or latchet gleamed with gold. So armed as he was he hearkened Mass and made his offering at the high altar. Then he came to the king, and the knights of his court, and courteously took leave of lords and ladies, and they kissed him, and commended him to Christ.

With that was Gringalet ready, girt with a saddle that gleamed gaily with many golden fringes, enriched and decked anew for the venture. The bridle was all barred about with bright gold buttons, and all the covertures and trappings of the steed, the crupper and the rich skirts, accorded with the saddle; spread fair with the rich red gold that glittered and gleamed in the rays of the sun.

Then the knight called for his helmet, which was well lined throughout, and set it high on his head, and hasped it behind. He wore a light kerchief over the vintail, that was broidered and studded with fair gems on a broad silken ribbon, with birds of gay colour, and many a turtle and true-lover's knot interlaced thickly, even as many a maiden had wrought diligently for seven winter long. But the circlet which crowned his helmet was yet more precious, being adorned with a device in diamonds. Then they brought him his shield, which was of bright red, with the pentangle painted thereon in gleaming gold. (7) And why that noble prince bare the pentangle I am minded to tell you, though my tale tarry thereby. It is a sign that Solomon set erewhile, as betokening truth; for it is a figure with five points and each line overlaps the other, and nowhere hath it beginning or end, so that in English it is called "the endless knot." And therefore was it well suiting to this knight and to his arms, since Gawain was faithful in five and five-fold, for pure was he as gold, void of all villainy and endowed with all virtues. Therefore he bare the pentangle on shield and surcoat as truest of heroes and gentlest of knights.

For first he was faultless in his five senses; and his five fingers never failed him; and all his trust upon earth was in the five wounds that Christ bare on the cross, as the Creed tells. And wherever this knight found himself in stress of battle he deemed well that he drew his strength from the five joys which the Queen of Heaven had of her Child. And for this cause did he bear an image of Our Lady on the one half of his shield, that whenever he looked upon it he might not lack for aid. And the fifth five that the hero used were frankness and fellowship above all, purity and courtesy that never failed him, and compassion that surpasses all; and in these five virtues was that hero wrapped and clothed. And all these, five-fold, were linked one in the other, so that they had no end, and were fixed on five points that never failed, neither at any side were they joined or sundered, nor could ye find beginning or end. And therefore on his shield was the knot shapen, red-gold upon red, which is the pure pentangle. Now was Sir Gawain ready, and he took his lance in hand, and bade them all Farewell, he deemed it had been for ever.

Then he smote the steed with his spurs, and sprang on his way, so that sparks flew from the stones after him. All that saw him were grieved at heart, and said one to the other, "By Christ, 'tis great pity that one of such noble life should be lost! I'faith, 'twere not easy to find his equal upon earth. The king had done better to have wrought more warily. Yonder knight should have been made a duke; a gallant leader of men is he, and such a fate had beseemed him better than to be hewn in pieces at the will of an elfish man, for mere pride. Who ever knew a king to take such counsel as to risk his knights on a Christmas jest?" Many were the tears that flowed from their eyes when that goodly knight rode from the hall. He made no delaying, but went his way swiftly, and rode many a wild road, as I heard say in the book.

So rode Sir Gawain through the realm of Logres, on an errand that he held for no jest. Often he lay companionless at night, and must lack the fare that he liked. No comrade had he save his steed, and none save God with whom to take counsel. At length he drew nigh to North Wales, and left the isles of Anglesey on his left hand, crossing over the fords by the foreland over at Holyhead, till he came into the wilderness of Wirral (8), where but few dwell who love God and man of true heart. And ever he asked, as he fared, of all whom he met, if they had heard any tidings of a Green Knight in the country thereabout, or of a Green Chapel? And all answered him, Nay, never in their lives had they seen any man of such a hue. And the knight wended his way by many a strange road and many a rugged path, and the fashion of his countenance changed full often ere he saw the Green Chapel.

Many a cliff did he climb in that unknown land, where afar from his friends he rode as a stranger. Never did he come to a stream or a ford but he found a foe before him, and that one so marvellous, so foul and fell, that it behoved him to fight. So many wonders did that knight behold, that it were too long to tell the tenth part of them. Sometimes he fought with dragons and wolves; sometimes with wild men that dwelt in the rocks; another while with bulls, and bears, and wild boars, or with giants of the high moorland that drew near to him. Had he not been a doughty knight, enduring, and of well-proved valour, and a servant of God, doubtless he had been slain, for he was oft in danger of death. Yet he cared not so much for the strife, what he deemed worse was when the cold clear water was shed from the clouds, and froze ere it fell on the fallow ground. More nights than enough he slept in his harness on the bare rocks, near slain with the sleet, while the stream leapt bubbling from the crest of the hills, and hung in hard icicles over his head.

Thus in peril and pain, and many a hardship, the knight rode alone till Christmas Eve, and in that tide he made his prayer to the Blessed Virgin that she would guide his steps and lead him to some dwelling. On that morning he rode by a hill, and came into a thick forest, wild and drear; on each side were high hills, and thick woods below them of great hoar oaks, a hundred together, of hazel and hawthorn with their trailing boughs intertwined, and rough ragged moss spreading everywhere. On the bare twigs the birds chirped piteously, for pain of the cold. The knight upon Gringalet rode lonely beneath them, through marsh and mire, much troubled at heart lest he should fail to see the service of the Lord, who on that self-same night was born of a maiden for the cure of our grief; and therefore he said, sighing, "I beseech Thee, Lord, and Mary Thy gentle Mother, for some shelter where I may hear Mass, and Thy mattins at morn. This I ask meekly, and thereto I pray my Paternoster, Ave, and Credo." Thus he rode praying, and lamenting his misdeeds, and he crossed himself, and said, "May the Cross of Christ speed me."

Now that knight had crossed himself but thrice ere he was aware in the wood of a dwelling within a moat, above a lawn, on a mound surrounded by many mighty trees that stood round the moat. 'Twas the fairest castle that ever a knight owned (9); built in a meadow with a park all about it, and a spiked palisade, closely driven, that enclosed the trees for more than two miles. The knight was ware of the hold from the side, as it shone through the oaks. Then he lifted off his helmet, and thanked Christ and S. Julian that they had courteously granted his prayer, and hearkened to his cry. "Now," quoth the knight, "I beseech ye, grant me fair hostel." Then he pricked Gringalet with his golden spurs, and rode gaily towards the great gate, and came swiftly to the bridge end.

The bridge was drawn up and the gates close shut; the walls were strong and thick, so that they might fear no tempest. The knight on his charger abode on the bank of the deep double ditch that surrounded the castle. The walls were set deep in the water, and rose aloft to a wondrous height; they were of hard hewn stone up to the corbels, which were adorned beneath the battlements with fair carvings, and turrets set in between with many a loophole; a better barbican Sir Gawain had never looked upon. And within he beheld the high hall, with its tower and many windows with carven cornices, and chalk-white chimneys on the turreted roofs that shone fair in the sun. And everywhere, thickly scattered on the castle battlements, were pinnacles, so many that it seemed as if it were all wrought out of paper, so white was it.

The knight on his steed deemed it fair enough, if he might come to be sheltered within it to lodge there while that the Holy-day lasted. He called aloud, and soon there came a porter of kindly countenance, who stood on the wall and greeted this knight and asked his errand.

"Good sir," quoth Gawain, "wilt thou go mine errand to the high lord of the castle, and crave for me lodging?"

"Yea, by S. Peter," quoth the porter. "In sooth I trow that ye be welcome to dwell here so long as it may like ye."

Then he went, and came again swiftly, and many folk with him to receive the knight. They let down the great drawbridge, and came forth and knelt on their knees on the cold earth to give him worthy welcome. They held wide open the great gates, and courteously he bid them rise, and rode over the bridge. Then men came to him and held his stirrup while he dismounted, and took and stabled his steed. There came down knights and squires to bring the guest with joy to the hall. When he raised his helmet there were many to take it from his hand, fain to serve him, and they took from him sword and shield.

Sir Gawain gave good greeting to the noble and the mighty men who came to do him honour. Clad in his shining armour they led him to the hall, where a great fire burnt brightly on the floor; and the lord of the household came forth from his chamber to meet the hero fitly. He spake to the knight, and said: "Ye are welcome to do here as it likes ye. All that is here is your own to have at your will and disposal."

"Gramercy!" quote Gawain, "may Christ requite ye."

As friends that were fain each embraced the other; and Gawain looked on the knight who greeted him so kindly, and thought 'twas a bold warrior that owned that burg.

Of mighty stature he was, and of high age; broad and flowing was his beard, and of a bright hue. He was stalwart of limb, and strong in his stride, his face fiery red, and his speech free: in sooth he seemed one well fitted to be a leader of valiant men.

Then the lord led Sir Gawain to a chamber, and commanded folk to wait upon him, and at his bidding there came men enough who brought the guest to a fair bower. The bedding was noble, with curtains of pure silk wrought with gold, and wondrous coverings of fair cloth all embroidered. The curtains ran on ropes with rings of red gold, and the walls were hung with carpets of Orient, and the same spread on the floor. There with mirthful speeches they took from the guest his byrny and all his shining armour, and brought him rich robes of the choicest in its stead. They were long and flowing, and became him well, and when he was clad in them all who looked on the hero thought that surely God had never made a fairer knight: he seemed as if he might be a prince without peer in the field where men strive in battle.

Then before the hearth-place, whereon the fire burned, they made ready a chair for Gawain, hung about with cloth and fair cushions; and there they cast around him a mantle of brown samite, richly embroidered and furred within with costly skins of ermine, with a hood of the same, and he seated himself in that rich seat, and warmed himself at the fire, and was cheered at heart. And while he sat thus the serving men set up a table on trestles, and covered it with a fair white cloth, and set thereon salt-cellar, and napkin, and silver spoons; and the knight washed at his will, and set him down to meat.

The folk served him courteously with many dishes seasoned of the best, a double portion. All kinds of fish were there, some baked in bread, some broiled on the embers, some sodden, some stewed and savoured with spices, with all sorts of cunning devices to his taste. And often he called it a feast, when they spake gaily to him all together, and said, "Now take ye this penance, and it shall be for your amendment." Much mirth thereof did Sir Gawain make.

Then they questioned that prince courteously of whence he came; and he told them that he was of the court of Arthur, who is the rich royal King of the Round Table, and that it was Gawain himself who was within their walls, and would keep Christmas with them, as the chance had fallen out. And when the lord of the castle heard those tidings he laughed aloud for gladness, and all men in that keep were joyful that they should be in the company of him to whom belonged all fame, and valour, and courtesy, and whose honour was praised above that of all men on earth. Each said softly to his fellow, "Now shall we see courteous bearing, and the manner of speech befitting courts. What charm lieth in gentle speech shall we learn without asking, since here we have welcomed the fine father of courtesy. God has surely shewn us His grace since He sends us such a guest as Gawain! When men shall sit and sing, blithe for Christ's birth, this knight shall bring us to the knowledge of fair manners, and it may be that hearing him we may learn the cunning speech of love."

By the time the knight had risen from dinner it was near nightfall. Then chaplains took their way to the chapel, and rang loudly, even as they should, for the solemn evensong of the high feast. Thither went the lord, and the lady also, and entered with her maidens into a comely closet, and thither also went Gawain. Then the lord took him by the sleeve and led him to a seat, and called him by his name, and told him he was of all men in the world the most welcome. And Sir Gawain thanked him truly, and each kissed the other, and they sat gravely together throughout the service.

Then was the lady fain to look upon that knight; and she came forth from her closet with many fair maidens. The fairest of ladies was she in face, and figure, and colouring, fairer even than Guinevere, so the knight thought. She came through the chancel to greet the hero, another lady held her by the left hand, older than she, and seemingly of high estate, with many nobles about her. But unlike to look upon were those ladies, for if the younger were fair, the elder was yellow. Rich red were the cheeks of the one, rough and wrinkled those of the other; the kerchiefs of the one were broidered with many glistening pearls, her throat and neck bare, and whiter than the snow that lies on the hills; the neck of the other was swathed in a gorget, with a white wimple over her black chin. Her forehead was wrapped in silk with many folds, worked with knots, so that naught of her was seen save her black brows, her eyes, her nose and her lips, and those were bleared, and ill to look upon. A worshipful lady in sooth one might call her! In figure was she short and broad, and thickly made--far fairer to behold was she whom she led by the hand.

When Gawain beheld that fair lady, who looked at him graciously, with leave of the lord he went towards them, and, bowing low, he greeted the elder, but the younger and fairer he took lightly in his arms, and kissed her courteously, and greeted her in knightly wise. Then she hailed him as friend, and he quickly prayed to be counted as her servant, if she so willed. Then they took him between them, and talking, led him to the chamber, to the hearth, and bade them bring spices, and they brought them in plenty with the good wine that was wont to be drunk at such seasons. Then the lord sprang to his feet and bade them make merry, and took off his hood, and hung it on a spear, and bade him win the worship thereof who should make most mirth that Christmas-tide. "And I shall try, by my faith, to fool it with the best, by the help of my friends, ere I lose my raiment." Thus with gay words the lord made trial to gladden Gawain with jests that night, till it was time to bid them light the tapers, and Sir Gawain took leave of them and gat him to rest.

In the morn when all men call to mind how Christ our Lord was born on earth to die for us, there is joy, for His sake, in all dwellings of the world; and so was there here on that day. For high feast was held, with many dainties and cunningly cooked messes. On the daïs sat gallant men, clad in their best. The ancient dame sat on the high seat, with the lord of the castle beside her. Gawain and the fair lady sat together, even in the midst of the board, when the feast was served; and so throughout all the hall each sat in his degree, and was served in order. There was meat, there was mirth, there was much joy, so that to tell thereof would take me too long, though peradventure I might strive to declare it. But Gawain and that fair lady had much joy of each other's company through her sweet words and courteous converse. And there was music made before each prince, trumpets and drums, and merry piping; each man hearkened his minstrel, and they too hearkened theirs.

So they held high feast that day and the next, and the third day thereafter, and the joy on S. John's Day was fair to hearken, for 'twas the last of the feast and the guests would depart in the grey of the morning. Therefore they awoke early, and drank wine, and danced fair carols, and at last, when it was late, each man took his leave to wend early on his way. Gawain would bid his host farewell, but the lord took him by the hand, and led him to his own chamber beside the hearth, and there he thanked him for the favour he had shown him in honouring his dwelling at that high season, and gladdening his castle with his fair countenance. "I wis, sir, that while I live I shall be held the worthier that Gawain has been my guest at God's own feast."

"Gramercy, sir," quoth Gawain, "in good faith, all the honour is yours, may the High King give it you, and I am but at your will to work your behest, inasmuch as I am beholden to you in great and small by rights."

Then the lord did his best to persuade the knight to tarry with him, but Gawain answered that he might in no wise do so. Then the host asked him courteously what stern behest had driven him at the holy season from the king's court, to fare all alone, ere yet the feast was ended?

"Forsooth," quoth the knight, "ye say but the truth: 'tis a high quest and a pressing that hath brought me afield, for I am summoned myself to a certain place, and I know not whither in the world I may wend to find it; so help me Christ, I would give all the kingdom of Logres an I might find it by New Year's morn. Therefore, sir, I make request of you that ye tell me truly if ye ever heard word of the Green Chapel, where it may be found, and the Green Knight that keeps it. For I am pledged by solemn compact sworn between us to meet that knight at the New Year if so I were on life; and of that same New Year it wants but little--I'faith, I would look on that hero more joyfully than on any other fair sight! Therefore, by your will, it behoves me to leave you, for I have but barely three days, and I would as fain fall dead as fail of mine errand."

Then the lord quoth, laughing, "Now must ye needs stay, for I will show you your goal, the Green Chapel, ere your term be at an end, have ye no fear! But ye can take your ease, friend, in your bed, till the fourth day, and go forth on the first of the year and come to that place at mid-morn to do as ye will. Dwell here till New Year's Day, and then rise and set forth, and ye shall be set in the way; 'tis not two miles hence."

Then was Gawain glad, and he laughed gaily. "Now I thank you for this above all else. Now my quest is achieved I will dwell here at your will, and otherwise do as ye shall ask."

Then the lord took him, and set him beside him, and bade the ladies be fetched for their greater pleasure, tho' between themselves they had solace. The lord, for gladness, made merry jest, even as one who wist not what to do for joy; and he cried aloud to the knight, "Ye have promised to do the thing I bid ye: will ye hold to this behest, here, at once?"

"Yea, forsooth," said that true knight, "while I abide in your burg I am bound by your behest."

"Ye have travelled from far," said the host, "and since then ye have waked with me, ye are not well refreshed by rest and sleep, as I know. Ye shall therefore abide in your chamber, and lie at your ease tomorrow at Mass-tide, and go to meat when ye will with my wife, who shall sit with you, and comfort you with her company till I return; and I shall rise early and go forth to the chase." And Gawain agreed to all this courteously.

"Sir knight," quoth the host, "we shall make a covenant. Whatsoever I win in the wood shall be yours, and whatever may fall to your share, that shall ye exchange for it. Let us swear, friend, to make this exchange, however our hap may be, for worse or for better."

"I grant ye your will," quoth Gawain the good; "if ye list so to do, it liketh me well."

"Bring hither the wine-cup, the bargain is made," so said the lord of that castle. They laughed each one, and drank of the wine, and made merry, these lords and ladies, as it pleased them. Then with gay talk and merry jest they arose, and stood, and spoke softly, and kissed courteously, and took leave of each other. With burning torches, and many a serving-man, was each led to his couch; yet ere they gat them to bed the old lord oft repeated their covenant, for he knew well how to make sport.

Full early, ere daylight, the folk rose up; the guests who would depart called their grooms, and they made them ready, and saddled the steeds, tightened up the girths, and trussed up their mails. The knights, all arrayed for riding, leapt up lightly, and took their bridles, and each rode his way as pleased him best.

The lord of the land was not the last. Ready for the chase, with many of his men, he ate a sop hastily when he had heard Mass, and then with blast of the bugle fared forth to the field. (10) He and his nobles were to horse ere daylight glimmered upon the earth.

Then the huntsmen coupled their hounds, unclosed the kennel door, and called them out. They blew three blasts gaily on the bugles, the hounds bayed fiercely, and they that would go a-hunting checked and chastised them. A hundred hunters there were of the best, so I have heard tell. Then the trackers gat them to the trysting-place and uncoupled the hounds, and forest rang again with their gay blasts.

At the first sound of the hunt the game quaked for fear, and fled, trembling, along the vale. They betook them to the heights, but the liers in wait turned them back with loud cries; the harts they let pass them, and the stags with their spreading antlers, for the lord had forbidden that they should be slain, but the hinds and the does they turned back, and drave down into the valleys. Then might ye see much shooting of arrows. As the deer fled under the boughs a broad whistling shaft smote and wounded each sorely, so that, wounded and bleeding, they fell dying on the banks. The hounds followed swiftly on their tracks, and hunters, blowing the horn, sped after them with ringing shouts as if the cliffs burst asunder. What game escaped those that shot was run down at the outer ring. Thus were they driven on the hills, and harassed at the waters, so well did the men know their work, and the greyhounds were so great and swift that they ran them down as fast as the hunters could slay them. Thus the lord passed the day in mirth and joyfulness, even to nightfall.

So the lord roamed the woods, and Gawain, that good night, lay ever a-bed, curtained about, under the costly coverlet, while the daylight gleamed on the walls. And as he lay half slumbering, he heard a little sound at the door, and he raised his head, and caught back a corner of the curtain, and waited to see what it might be. It was the lovely lady, the lord's wife; she shut the door softly behind her, and turned towards the bed; and Gawain was shamed, laid him down softly and made as if he slept. And she came lightly to the bedside, within the curtain, and sat herself down beside him, to wait till he wakened. The knight lay there awhile, and marvelled within himself what her coming might betoken; and he said to himself, "'Twere more seemly if I asked her what hath brought her hither." Then he made feint to waken, and turned towards her, and opened his eyes as one astonished, and crossed himself; and she looked on him laughing, with her cheeks red and white, lovely to behold, and small smiling lips.

"Good morrow, Sir Gawain," said that fair lady; "ye are but a careless sleeper, since one can enter thus. Now are ye taken unawares, and lest ye escape me I shall bind you in your bed; of that be ye assured!" Laughing, she spake these words.

"Good morrow, fair lady," quoth Gawain blithely. "I will do your will, as it likes me well. For I yield me readily, and pray your grace, and that is best, by my faith, since I needs must do so." Thus he jested again, laughing. "But an ye would, fair lady, grant me this grace that ye pray your prisoner to rise. I would get me from bed, and array me better, then could I talk with ye in more comfort."

"Nay, forsooth, fair sir," quoth the lady, "ye shall not rise, I will rede ye better. I shall keep ye here, since ye can do no other, and talk with my knight whom I have captured. For I know well that ye are Sir Gawain, whom all the world worships, wheresoever ye may ride. Your honour and your courtesy are praised by lords and ladies, by all who live. Now ye are here and we are alone, my lord and his men are afield; the serving men in their beds, and my maidens also, and the door shut upon us. And since in this hour I have him that all men love, I shall use my time well with speech, while it lasts. Ye are welcome to my company, for it behoves me in sooth to be your servant."

"In good faith," quoth Gawain, "I think me that I am not him of whom ye speak, for unworthy am I of such service as ye here proffer. In sooth, I were glad if I might set myself by word or service to your pleasure; a pure joy would it be to me!"

"In good faith, Sir Gawain," quoth the gay lady, "the praise and the prowess that pleases all ladies I lack them not, nor hold them light; yet are there ladies enough who would liever now have the knight in their hold, as I have ye here, to dally with your courteous words, to bring them comfort and to ease their cares, than much of the treasure and the gold that are theirs. And now, through the grace of Him who upholds the heavens, I have wholly in my power that which they all desire!"

Thus the lady, fair to look upon, made him great cheer, and Sir Gawain, with modest words, answered her again: "Madam," he quoth, "may Mary requite ye, for in good faith I have found in ye a noble frankness. Much courtesy have other folk shown me, but the honour they have done me is naught to the worship of yourself, who knoweth but good."

"By Mary," quoth the lady, "I think otherwise; for were I worth all the women alive, and had I the wealth of the world in my hand, and might choose me a lord to my liking, then, for all that I have seen in ye, Sir Knight, of beauty and courtesy and blithe semblance, and for all that I have hearkened and hold for true, there should be no knight on earth to be chosen before ye!"

"Well I wot," quoth Sir Gawain, "that ye have chosen a better; but I am proud that ye should so prize me, and as your servant do I hold ye my sovereign, and your knight am I, and may Christ reward ye."

So they talked of many matters till mid-morn was past, and ever the lady made as though she loved him, and the knight turned her speech aside. For though she were the brightest of maidens, yet had he forborne to shew her love for the danger that awaited him, and the blow that must be given without delay.

Then the lady prayed her leave from him, and he granted it readily. And she gave [the text reads "have"] him good-day, with laughing glance, but he must needs marvel at her words:

"Now He that speeds fair speech reward ye this disport; but that ye be Gawain my mind misdoubts me greatly."

"Wherefore?" quoth the knight quickly, fearing lest he had lacked in some courtesy.

And the lady spake: "So true a knight as Gawain is holden, and one so perfect in courtesy, would never have tarried so long with a lady but he would of his courtesy have craved a kiss at parting."

Then quoth Gawain, "I wot I will do even as it may please ye, and kiss at your commandment, as a true knight should who forbears to ask for fear of displeasure."

At that she came near and bent down and kissed the knight, and each commended the other to Christ, and she went forth from the chamber softly.

Then Sir Gawain arose and called his chamberlain and chose his garments, and when he was ready he gat him forth to Mass, and then went to meat, and made merry all day till the rising of the moon, and never had a knight fairer lodging than had he with those two noble ladies, the elder and the younger.

And even the lord of the land chased the hinds through holt and heath till eventide, and then with much blowing of bugles and baying of hounds they bore the game homeward; and by the time daylight was done all the folk had returned to that fair castle. And when the lord and Sir Gawain met together, then were they both well pleased. The lord commanded them all to assemble in the great hall, and the ladies to descend with their maidens, and there, before them all, he bade the men fetch in the spoil of the day's hunting, and he called unto Gawain, and counted the tale of the beasts, and showed them unto him, and said, "What think ye of this game, Sir Knight? Have I deserved of ye thanks for my woodcraft?"

"Yea, I wis," quoth the other, "here is the fairest spoil I have seen this seven year in the winter season."

"And all this do I give ye, Gawain," quoth the host, "for by accord of covenant ye may claim it as your own."

"That is sooth," quoth the other, "I grant you that same; and I have fairly won this within walls, and with as good will do I yield it to ye." With that he clasped his hands round the lord's neck and kissed him as courteously as he might. "Take ye here my spoils, no more have I won; ye should have it freely, though it were greater than this."

"'Tis good," said the host, "gramercy thereof. Yet were I fain to know where ye won this same favour, and if it were by your own wit?"

"Nay," answered Gawain, "that was not in the bond. Ask me no more: ye have taken what was yours by right, be content with that."

They laughed and jested together, and sat them down to supper, where they were served with many dainties; and after supper they sat by the hearth, and wine was served out to them; and oft in their jesting they promised to observe on the morrow the same covenant that they had made before, and whatever chance might betide to exchange their spoil, be it much or little, when they met at night. Thus they renewed their bargain before the whole court, and then the night-drink was served, and each courteously took leave of the other and gat him to bed.

By the time the cock had crowed thrice the lord of the castle had left his bed; Mass was sung and meat fitly served. The folk were forth to the wood ere the day broke, with hound and horn they rode over the plain, and uncoupled their dogs among the thorns. Soon they struck on the scent, and the hunt cheered on the hounds who were first to seize it, urging them with shouts. The others hastened to the cry, forty at once, and there rose such a clamour from the pack that the rocks rang again. The huntsmen spurred them on with shouting and blasts of the horn; and the hounds drew together to a thicket betwixt the water and a high crag in the cliff beneath the hillside. There where the rough rock fell ruggedly they, the huntsmen, fared to the finding, and cast about round the hill and the thicket behind them. The knights wist well what beast was within, and would drive him forth with the bloodhounds. And as they beat the bushes, suddenly over the beaters there rushed forth a wondrous great and fierce boar, long since had he left the herd to roam by himself. Grunting, he cast many to the ground, and fled forth at his best speed, without more mischief. The men hallooed loudly and cried, "Hay! Hay!" and blew the horns to urge on the hounds, and rode swiftly after the boar. Many a time did he turn to bay and tare the hounds, and they yelped, and howled shrilly. Then the men made ready their arrows and shot at him, but the points were turned on his thick hide, and the barbs would not bite upon him, for the shafts shivered in pieces, and the head but leapt again wherever it hit.

But when the boar felt the stroke of the arrows he waxed mad with rage, and turned on the hunters and tare many, so that, affrightened, they fled before him. But the lord on a swift steed pursued him, blowing his bugle; as a gallant knight he rode through the woodland chasing the boar till the sun grew low.

So did the hunters this day, while Sir Gawain lay in his bed lapped in rich gear; and the lady forgat not to salute him, for early was she at his side, to cheer his mood.

She came to the bedside and looked on the knight, and Gawain gave her fit greeting, and she greeted him again with ready words, and sat her by his side and laughed, and with a sweet look she spoke to him:

"Sir, if ye be Gawain, I think it a wonder that ye be so stern and cold, and care not for the courtesies of friendship, but if one teach ye to know them ye cast the lesson out of your mind. Ye have soon forgotten what I taught ye yesterday, by all the truest tokens that I knew!"

"What is that?" quoth the knight. "I trow I know not. If it be sooth that ye say, then is the blame mine own."

"But I taught ye of kissing, " quoth the fair lady. "Wherever a fair countenance is shown him, it behoves a courteous knight quickly to claim a kiss."

"Nay, my dear," said Sir Gawain, "cease that speech; that durst I not do lest I were denied, for if I were forbidden I wot I were wrong did I further entreat."

"I' faith," quoth the lady merrily, "ye may not be forbid, ye are strong enough to constrain by strength an ye will, were any so discourteous as to give ye denial."

"Yea, by Heaven," said Gawain, "ye speak well; but threats profit little in the land where I dwell, and so with a gift that is given not of good will! I am at your commandment to kiss when ye like, to take or to leave as ye list."

Then the lady bent her down and kissed him courteously.

And as they spake together she said, "I would learn somewhat from ye, an ye would not be wroth, for young ye bare and fair, and so courteous and knightly as ye are known to be, the head of all chivalry, and versed in all wisdom of love and war-- 'tis ever told of true knights how they adventured their lives for their true love, and endured hardships for her favours, and avenged her with valour, and eased her sorrows, and brought joy to her bower; and ye are the fairest knight of your time, and your fame and your honour are everywhere, yet I have sat by ye here twice, and never a word have I heard of love! Ye who are so courteous and skilled in such love ought surely to teach one so young and unskilled some little craft of true love! Why are ye so unlearned who art otherwise so famous? Or is it that ye deemed me unworthy to hearken to your teaching? For shame, Sir Knight! I come hither alone and sit at your side to learn of ye some skill; teach me of your wit, while my lord is from home."

"In good faith," quoth Gawain, "great is my joy and my profit that so fair a lady as ye are should deign to come hither, and trouble ye with so poor a man, and make sport with your knight with kindly countenance, it pleaseth me much. But that I, in my turn, should take it upon me to tell of love and such like matters to ye who know more by half, or a hundred fold, of such craft than I do, or ever shall in all my lifetime, by my troth 'twere folly indeed! I will work your will to the best of my might as I am bounden, and evermore will I be your servant, so help me Christ!"

Then often with guile she questioned that knight that she might win him to woo her, but he defended himself so fairly that none might in any wise blame him, and naught but bliss and harmless jesting was there between them. They laughed and talked together till at last she kissed him, and craved her leave of him, and went her way.

Then the knight arose and went forth to Mass, and afterward dinner was served and he sat and spake with the ladies all day. But the lord of the castle rode ever over the land chasing the wild boar, that fled through the thickets, slaying the best of his hounds and breaking their backs in sunder; till at last he was so weary he might run no longer, but made for a hole in a mound by a rock. He got the mound at his back and faced the hounds, whetting his white tusks and foaming at the mouth. The huntsmen stood aloof, fearing to draw nigh him; so many of them had been already wounded that they were loth to be torn with his tusks, so fierce he was and mad with rage. At length the lord himself came up, and saw the beast at bay, and the men standing aloof.

Then quickly he sprang to the ground and drew out a bright blade, and waded through the stream to the boar.

When the beast was aware of the knight with weapon in hand, he set up his bristles and snorted loudly, and many feared for their lord lest he should be slain. Then the boar leapt upon the knight so that beast and man were one atop of the other in the water; but the boar had the worst of it, for the man had marked, even as he sprang, and set the point of his brand to the beast's chest, and drove it up to the hilt, so that the heart was split in twain, and the boar fell snarling, and was swept down by the water to where a hundred hounds seized on him, and the men drew him to shore for the dogs to slay.

Then was there loud blowing of horns and baying of hounds, the huntsmen smote off the boar's head, and hung the carcase by the four feet to a stout pole, and so went on their way homewards. The head they bore before the lord himself, who had slain the beast at the ford by force of his strong hand.

It seemed him o'er long ere he saw Sir Gawain in the hall, and he called, and the guest came to take that which fell to his share. And when he saw Gawain the lord laughed aloud, and bade them call the ladies and the household together, and he showed them the game, and told them the tale, how they hunted the wild boar through the woods, and of his length and breadth and height; and Sir Gawain commended his deeds and praised him for his valour, well proven, for so mighty a beast had he never seen before.

Then they handled the huge head, and the lord said aloud, "Now, Gawain, this game is your own by sure covenant, as ye right well know."

"'Tis sooth," quoth the knight, "and as truly will I give ye all I have gained." He took the host round the neck, and kissed him courteously twice. "Now are we quits," he said, "this eventide, of all the covenants that we made since I came hither."

And the lord answered, "By S. Giles, ye are the best I know; ye will be rich in a short space if ye drive such bargains!"

Then they set up the tables on trestles, and covered them with fair cloths, and lit waxen tapers on the walls. The knights sat and were served in the hall, and much game and glee was there round the hearth, with many songs, both at supper and after; song of Christmas, and new carols, with all the mirth one may think of. And ever that lovely lady sat by the knight, and with still stolen looks made such feint of pleasing him, that Gawain marvelled much, and was wroth with himself, but he could not for his courtesy return her fair glances, but dealt with her cunningly, however she might strive to wrest the thing.

When they had tarried in the hall so long as it seemed them good, they turned to the inner chamber and the wide hearthplace, and there they drank wine, and the host proffered to renew the covenant for New Year's Eve; but the knight craved leave to depart on the morrow, for it was nigh to the term when he must fulfil his pledge. But the lord would withhold him from so doing, and prayed him to tarry, and said,

"As I am a true knight I swear my troth that ye shall come to the Green Chapel to achieve your task on New Year's morn, long before prime. Therefore abide ye in your bed, and I will hunt in this wood, and hold ye to the covenant to exchange with me against all the spoil I may bring hither. For twice have I tried ye, and found ye true, and the morrow shall be the third time and the best. Make we merry now while we may, and think on joy, for misfortune may take a man whensoever it wills."

Then Gawain granted his request, and they brought them drink, and they gat them with lights to bed.

Sir Gawain lay and slept softly, but the lord, who was keen on woodcraft, was afoot early. After Mass he and his men ate a morsel, and he asked for his steed; all the knights who should ride with him were already mounted before the hall gates.

'Twas a fair frosty morning, for the sun rose red in ruddy vapour, and the welkin was clear of clouds. The hunters scattered them by a forest side, and the rocks rang again with the blast of their horns. Some came on the scent of a fox, and a hound gave tongue; the huntsmen shouted, and the pack followed in a crowd on the trail. The fox ran before them, and when they saw him they pursued him with noise and much shouting, and he wound and turned through many a thick grove, often cowering and hearkening in a hedge. At last by a little ditch he leapt out of a spinney, stole away slily by a copse path, and so out of the wood and away from the hounds. But he went, ere he wist, to a chosen tryst, and three started forth on him at once, so he must needs double back, and betake him to the wood again.

Then was it joyful to hearken to the hounds; when all the pack had met together and had sight of their game they made as loud a din as if all the lofty cliffs had fallen clattering together. The huntsmen shouted and threatened, and followed close upon him so that he might scarce escape, but Reynard was wily, and he turned and doubled upon them, and led the lord and his men over the hills, now on the slopes, now in the vales, while the knight at home slept through the cold morning beneath his costly curtains.

But the fair lady of the castle rose betimes, and clad herself in a rich mantle that reached even to the ground, left her throat and her fair neck bare, and was bordered and lined with costly furs. On her head she wore no golden circlet, but a network of precious stones, that gleamed and shone through her tresses in clusters of twenty together. Thus she came into the chamber, closed the door after her, and set open a window, and called to him gaily, "Sir Knight, how may ye sleep? The morning is so fair."

Sir Gawain was deep in slumber, and in his dream he vexed him much for the destiny that should befall him on the morrow, when he should meet the knight at the Green Chapel, and abide his blow; but when the lady spake he heard her, and came to himself, and roused from his dream and answered swiftly. The lady came laughing, and kissed him courteously, and he welcomed her fittingly with a cheerful countenance. He saw her so glorious and gaily dressed, so faultless of features and complexion, that it warmed his heart to look upon her.

They spake to each other smiling, and all was bliss and good cheer between them. They exchanged fair words, and much happiness was therein, yet was there a gulf between them, and she might win no more of her knight, for that gallant prince watched well his words--he would neither take her love, nor frankly refuse it. He cared for his courtesy, lest he be deemed churlish, and yet more for his honour lest he be traitor to his host. "God forbid," quoth he to himself, "that it should so befall." Thus with courteous words did he set aside all the special speeches that came from her lips.

Then spake the lady to the knight, "Ye deserve blame if ye hold not that lady who sits beside ye above all else in the world, if ye have not already a love whom ye hold dearer, and like better, and have sworn such firm faith to that lady that ye care not to loose it--and that am I now fain to believe. And now I pray ye straitly that ye tell me that in truth, and hide it not."

And the knight answered, "By S. John" (and he smiled as he spake) "no such love have I, nor do I think to have yet awhile."

"That is the worst word I may hear," quoth the lady, "but in sooth I have mine answer; kiss me now courteously, and I will go hence; I can but mourn as a maiden that loves much."

Sighing, she stooped down and kissed him, and then she rose up and spake as she stood, "Now, dear, at our parting do me this grace: give me some gift, if it were but thy glove, that I may bethink me of my knight, and lessen my mourning."

"Now, I wis," quoth the knight, "I would that I had here the most precious thing that I possess on earth that I might leave ye as love-token, great or small, for ye have deserved forsooth more reward than I might give ye. But it is not to your honour to have at this time a glove for reward as gift from Gawain, and I am here on a strange errand, and have no man with me, nor mails with goodly things--that mislikes me much, lady, at this time; but each man must fare as he is taken, if for sorrow and ill."

"Nay, knight highly honoured," quoth that lovesome lady, "though I have naught of yours, yet shall ye have somewhat of mine." With that she reached him a ring of red gold with a sparkling stone therein, that shone even as the sun (wit ye well, it was worth many marks); but the knight refused it, and spake readily,

"I will take no gift, lady, at this time. I have none to give, and none will I take."

She prayed him to take it, but he refused her prayer, and sware in sooth that he would not have it.

The lady was sorely vexed, and said, "If ye refuse my ring as too costly, that ye will not be so highly beholden to me, I will give you my girdle (11) as a lesser gift." With that she loosened a lace that was fastened at her side, knit upon her kirtle under her mantle. It was wrought of green silk, and gold, only braided by the fingers, and that she offered to the knight, and besought him though it were of little worth that he would take it, and he said nay, he would touch neither gold nor gear ere God give him grace to achieve the adventure for which he had come hither. "And therefore, I pray ye, displease ye not, and ask me no longer, for I may not grant it. I am dearly beholden to ye for the favour ye have shown me, and ever, in heat and cold, will I be your true servant."

"Now," said the lady, "ye refuse this silk, for it is simple in itself, and so it seems, indeed; lo, it is small to look upon and less in cost, but whoso knew the virtue that is knit therein he would, peradventure, value it more highly. For whatever knight is girded with this green lace, while he bears it knotted about him there is no man under heaven can overcome him, for he may not be slain for any magic on earth."

Then Gawain bethought him, and it came into his heart that this were a jewel for the jeopardy that awaited him when he came to the Green Chapel to seek the return blow--could he so order it that he should escape unslain, 'twere a craft worth trying.

Then he bare with her chiding, and let her say her say, and she pressed the girdle on him and prayed him to take it, and he granted her prayer, and she gave it him with good will, and besought him for her sake never to reveal it but to hide it loyally from her lord; and the knight agreed that never should any man know it, save they two alone. He thanked her often and heartily, and she kissed him for the third time.

Then she took her leave of him, and when she was gone Sir Gawain arose, and clad him in rich attire, and took the girdle, and knotted it round him, and hid it beneath his robes. Then he took his way to the chapel, and sought out a priest privily and prayed him to teach him better how his soul might be saved when he should go hence; and there he shrived him, and showed his misdeeds, both great and small, and besought mercy and craved absolution; and the priest assoiled him, and set him as clean as if Doomsday had been on the morrow. And afterwards Sir Gawain made him merry with the ladies, with carols, and all kinds of joy, as never he did but that one day, even to nightfall; and all the men marvelled at him, and said that never since he came thither had he been so merry.

Meanwhile the lord of the castle was abroad chasing the fox; awhile he lost him, and as he rode through a spinny he heard the hounds near at hand, and Reynard came creeping through a thick grove, with all the pack at his heels. Then the lord drew out his shining brand, and cast it at the beast, and the fox swerved aside for the sharp edge, and would have doubled back, but a hound was on him ere he might turn, and right before the horse's feet they all fell on him, and worried him fiercely, snarling the while.

Then the lord leapt from his saddle, and caught the fox from the jaws, and held it aloft over his head, and hallooed loudly, and many brave hounds bayed as they beheld it; and the hunters hied them thither, blowing their horns; all that bare bugles blew them at once, and all the others shouted. 'Twas the merriest meeting that ever men heard, the clamour that was raised at the death of the fox. They rewarded the hounds, stroking them and rubbing their heads, and took Reynard and stripped him of his coat; then blowing their horns, they turned them homewards, for it was nigh nightfall.

The lord was gladsome at his return, and found a bright fire on the hearth, and the knight beside it, the good Sir Gawain, who was in joyous mood for the pleasure he had had with the ladies. He wore a robe of blue, that reached even to the ground, and a surcoat richly furred, that became him well. A hood like to the surcoat fell on his shoulders, and all alike were done about with fur. He met the host in the midst of the floor, and jesting, he greeted him, and said, "Now shall I be first to fulfil our covenant which we made together when there was no lack of wine." Then he embraced the knight, and kissed him thrice, as solemnly as he might.

"Of a sooth," quoth the other, "ye have good luck in the matter of this covenant, if ye made a good exchange!"

"Yea, it matters naught of the exchange," quoth Gawain, "since what I owe is swiftly paid."

"Marry," said the other, "mine is behind, for I have hunted all this day, and naught have I got but this foul fox-skin, and that is but poor payment for three such kisses as ye have here given me."

"Enough," quoth Sir Gawain, "I thank ye, by the Rood."

Then the lord told them of his hunting, and how the fox had been slain.

With mirth and minstrelsy, and dainties at their will, they made them as merry as a folk well might till 'twas time for them to sever, for at last they must needs betake them to their beds. Then the knight took his leave of the lord, and thanked him fairly.

"For the fair sojourn that I have had here at this high feast may the High King give ye honour. I give ye myself, as one of your servants, if ye so like; for I must needs, as you know, go hence with the morn, and ye will give me, as ye promised, a guide to show me the way to the Green Chapel, an God will suffer me on New Year's Day to deal the doom of my weird."

"By my faith," quoth the host, "all that ever I promised, that shall I keep with good will." Then he gave him a servant to set him in the way, and lead him by the downs, that he should have no need to ford the stream, and should fare by the shortest road through the groves; and Gawain thanked the lord for the honour done him. Then he would take leave of the ladies, and courteously he kissed them, and spake, praying them to receive his thanks, and they made like reply; then with many sighs they commended him to Christ, and he departed courteously from that folk. Each man that he met he thanked him for his service and his solace, and the pains he had been at to do his will; and each found it as hard to part from the knight as if he had ever dwelt with him.

Then they led him with torches to his chamber, and brought him to his bed to rest. That he slept soundly I may not say, for the morrow gave him much to think on. Let him rest awhile, for he was near that which he sought, and if ye will but listen to me I will tell ye how it fared with him thereafter.

Now the New Year drew nigh, and the night passed, and the day chased the darkness, as is God's will; but wild weather wakened therewith. The clouds cast the cold to the earth, with enough of the north to slay them that lacked clothing. The snow drave smartly, and the whistling wind blew from the heights, and made great drifts in the valleys. The knight, lying in his bed, listened, for though his eyes were shut, he might sleep but little, and hearkened every cock that crew.

He arose ere the day broke, by the light of a lamp that burned in his chamber, and called to his chamberlain, bidding him bring his armour and saddle his steed. The other gat him up, and fetched his garments, and robed Sir Gawain.

First he clad him in his clothes to keep off the cold, and then in his harness, which was well and fairly kept. Both hauberk and plates were well burnished, the rings of the rich byrny freed from rust, and all as fresh as at first, so that the knight was fain to thank them. Then he did on each piece, and bade them bring his steed, while he put the fairest raiment on himself; his coat with its fair cognizance, adorned with precious stones upon velvet, with broidered seams, and all furred within with costly skins. And he left not the lace, the lady's gift, that Gawain forgot not, for his own good. When he had girded on his sword he wrapped the gift twice about him, swathed around his waist. The girdle of green silk set gaily and well upon the royal red cloth, rich to behold, but the knight ware it not for pride of the pendants, polished though they were with fair gold that gleamed brightly on the ends, but to save himself from sword and knife, when it behoved him to abide his hurt without question. With that the hero went forth, and thanked that kindly folk full often.

Then was Gringalet ready, that was great and strong, and had been well cared for and tended in every wise; in fair condition was that proud steed, and fit for a journey. Then Gawain went to him, and looked on his coat, and said by his sooth, "There is a folk in this place that thinketh on honour; much joy may they have, and the lord who maintains them, and may all good betide that lovely lady all her life long. Since they for charity cherish a guest, and hold honour in their hands, may He who holds the heaven on high requite them, and also ye all. And if I might live anywhere on earth, I would give ye full reward, readily, if so I might." Then he set foot in the stirrup and bestrode his steed, and his squire gave him his shield, which he laid on his shoulder. Then he smote Gringalet with his golden spurs, and the steed pranced on the stones and would stand no longer.

By that his man was mounted, who bare his spear and lance, and Gawain quoth, "I commend this castle to Christ, may He give it ever good fortune." Then the drawbridge was let down, and the broad gates unbarred and opened on both sides; the knight crossed himself, and passed through the gateway, and praised the porter, who knelt before the prince, and gave him good-day, and commended him to God. Thus the knight went on his way with the one man who should guide him to that dread place where he should receive rueful payment.

The two went by hedges where the boughs were bare, and climbed the cliffs where the cold clings. Naught fell from the heavens, but 'twas ill beneath them; mist brooded over the moor and hung on the mountains; each hill had a cap, a great cloak, of mist. The streams foamed and bubbled between their banks, dashing sparkling on the shores where they shelved downwards. Rugged and dangerous was the way through the woods, till it was time for the sun-rising. Then were they on a high hill; the snow lay white beside them, and the man who rode with Gawain drew rein by his master.

"Sir," he said, "I have brought ye hither, and now ye are not far from the place that ye have sought so specially. But I will tell ye for sooth, since I know ye well, and ye are such a knight as I well love, would ye follow my counsel ye would fare the better. The place whither ye go is accounted full perilous, for he who liveth in that waste is the worst on earth, for he is strong and fierce, and loveth to deal mighty blows; taller is he than any man on earth, and greater of frame than any four in Arthur's court, or in any other. And this is his custom at the Green Chapel; there may no man pass by that place, however proud his arms, but he does him to death by force of his hand, for he is a discourteous knight, and shews no mercy. Be he churl or chaplain who rides by that chapel, monk or mass priest, or any man else, he thinks it as pleasant to slay them as to pass alive himself. Therefore, I tell ye, as sooth as ye sit in saddle, if ye come there and that knight know it, ye shall be slain, though ye had twenty lives; trow me that truly! He has dwelt here full long and seen many a combat; ye may not defend ye against his blows. Therefore, good Sir Gawain, let the man be, and get ye away some other road; for God's sake seek ye another land, and there may Christ speed ye! And I will hie me home again, and I promise ye further that I will swear by God and the saints, or any other oath ye please, that I will keep counsel faithfully, and never let any wit the tale that ye fled for fear of any man."

"Gramercy," quoth Gawain, but ill-pleased. "Good fortune be his who wishes me good, and that thou wouldst keep faith with me I will believe; but didst thou keep it never so truly, an I passed here and fled for fear as thou sayest, then were I a coward knight, and might not be held guiltless. So I will to the chapel let chance what may, and talk with that man, even as I may list, whether for weal or for woe as fate may have it. Fierce though he may be in fight, yet God knoweth well how to save His servants."

"Well," quoth the other, "now that ye have said so much that ye will take your own harm on yourself, and ye be pleased to lose your life, I will neither let nor keep ye. Have here your helm and the spear in your hand, and ride down this same road beside the rock till ye come to the bottom of the valley, and there look a little to the left hand, and ye shall see in that vale the chapel, and the grim man who keeps it. Now fare ye well, noble Gawain; for all the gold on earth I would not go with ye nor bear ye fellowship one step further." With that the man turned his bridle into the wood, smote the horse with his spurs as hard as he could, and galloped off, leaving the knight alone.

Quoth Gawain, "I will neither greet nor groan, but commend myself to God, and yield me to His will."

Then the knight spurred Gringalet, and rode adown the path close in by a bank beside a grove. So he rode through the rough thicket, right into the dale, and there he halted, for it seemed him wild enough. No sign of a chapel could he see, but high and burnt banks on either side and rough rugged crags with great stones above. An ill-looking place he thought it.

Then he drew in his horse and looked around to seek the chapel, but he saw none and thought it strange. Then he saw as it were a mound on a level space of land by a bank beside the stream where it ran swiftly, the water bubbled within as if boiling. The knight turned his steed to the mound, and lighted down and tied the rein to the branch of a linden; and he turned to the mound and walked round it, questioning with himself what it might be. It had a hole at the end and at either side, and was overgrown with clumps of grass, and it was hollow within as an old cave or the crevice of a crag; he knew not what it might be.

"Ah," quoth Gawain, "can this be the Green Chapel? Here might the devil say his mattins at midnight! Now I wis there is wizardry here. 'Tis an ugly oratory, all overgrown with grass, and 'twould well beseem that fellow in green to say his devotions on devil's wise. Now feel I in five wits, 'tis the foul fiend himself who hath set me this tryst, to destroy me here! This is a chapel of mischance: ill-luck betide it, 'tis the cursedest kirk that ever I came in!"

Helmet on head and lance in hand, he came up to the rough dwelling, when he heard over the high hill beyond the brook, as it were in a bank, a wondrous fierce noise, that rang in the cliff as if it would cleave asunder. 'Twas as if one ground a scythe on a grindstone, it whirred and whetted like water on a mill-wheel and rushed and rang, terrible to hear.

"By God," quoth Gawain, "I trow that gear is preparing for the knight who will meet me here. Alas! naught may help me, yet should my life be forfeit, I fear not a jot!" With that he called aloud. "Who waiteth in this place to give me tryst? Now is Gawain come hither: if any man will aught of him let him hasten hither now or never."

"Stay," quoth one on the bank above his head, "and ye shall speedily have that which I promised ye." Yet for a while the noise of whetting went on ere he appeared, and then he came forth from a cave in the crag with a fell weapon, a Danish axe newly dight, wherewith to deal the blow. An evil head it had, four feet large, no less, sharply ground, and bound to the handle by the lace that gleamed brightly. And the knight himself was all green as before, face and foot, locks and beard, but now he was afoot. When he came to the water he would not wade it, but sprang over with the pole of his axe, and strode boldly over the brent that was white with snow.

Sir Gawain went to meet him, but he made no low bow. The other said, "Now, fair sir, one may trust thee to keep tryst. Thou art welcome, Gawain, to my place. Thou hast timed thy coming as befits a true man. Thou knowest the covenant set between us: at this time twelve months agone thou didst take that which fell to thee, and I at this New Year will readily requite thee. We are in this valley, verily alone, here are no knights to sever us, do what we will. Have off thy helm from thine head, and have here thy pay; make me no more talking than I did then when thou didst strike off my head with one blow."

"Nay," quoth Gawain, "by God that gave me life, I shall make no moan whatever befall me, but make thou ready for the blow and I shall stand still and say never a word to thee, do as thou wilt."

With that he bent his head and shewed his neck all bare, and made as if he had no fear, for he would not be thought a-dread.

Then the Green Knight made him ready, and grasped his grim weapon to smite Gawain. With all his force he bore it aloft with a mighty feint of slaying him: had it fallen as straight as he aimed he who was ever doughty of deed had been slain by the blow. But Gawain swerved aside as the axe came gliding down to slay him as he stood, and shrank a little with the shoulders, for the sharp iron. The other heaved up the blade and rebuked the prince with many proud words:

"Thou art not Gawain," he said, "who is held so valiant, that never feared he man by hill or vale, but thou shrinkest for fear ere thou feelest hurt. Such cowardice did I never hear of Gawain! Neither did I flinch from thy blow, or make strife in King Arthur's hall. My head fell to my feet, and yet I fled not; but thou didst wax faint of heart ere any harm befell. Wherefore must I be deemed the braver knight."

Quoth Gawain, "I shrank once, but so will I no more, though an my head fall on the stones I cannot replace it. But haste, Sir Knight, by thy faith, and bring me to the point, deal me my destiny, and do it out of hand, for I will stand thee a stroke and move no more till thine axe have hit me--my troth on it."

"Have at thee, then," quoth the other, and heaved aloft the axe with fierce mien, as if he were mad. He struck at him fiercely but wounded him not, withholding his hand ere it might strike him.

Gawain abode the stroke, and flinched in no limb, but stood still as a stone or the stump of a tree that is fast rooted in the rocky ground with a hundred roots.

Then spake gaily the man in green, "So now thou hast thine heart whole it behoves me to smite. Hold aside thy hood that Arthur gave thee, and keep thy neck thus bent lest it cover it again."

Then Gawain said angrily, "Why talk on thus? Thou dost threaten too long. I hope thy heart misgives thee."

"For sooth," quoth the other, "so fiercely thou speakest I will no longer let thine errand wait its reward." Then he braced himself to strike, frowning with lips and brow, 'twas no marvel that it pleased but ill him who hoped for no rescue. He lifted the axe lightly and let it fall with the edge of the blade on the bare neck. Though he struck swiftly it hurt him no more than on the one side where it severed the skin. The sharp blade cut into the flesh so that the blood ran over his shoulder to the ground. And when the knight saw the blood staining the snow, he sprang forth, swift-foot, more than a spear's length, seized his helmet and set it on his head, cast his shield over his shoulder, drew out his bright sword, and spake boldly (never since he was born was he half so blithe), "Stop, Sir Knight, bid me no more blows. I have stood a stroke here without flinching, and if thou give me another, I shall requite thee, and give thee as good again. By the covenant made betwixt us in Arthur's hall but one blow falls to me here. Halt, therefore."

Then the Green Knight drew off from him and leaned on his axe, setting the shaft on the ground, and looked on Gawain as he stood all armed and faced him fearlessly-- at heart it pleased him well. Then he spake merrily in a loud voice, and said to the knight, "Bold sir, be not so fierce, no man here hath done thee wrong, nor will do, save by covenant, as we made at Arthur's court. I promised thee a blow and thou hast it-- hold thyself well paid! I release thee of all other claims. If I had been so minded I might perchance have given thee a rougher buffet. First I menaced thee with a feigned one, and hurt thee not for the covenant that we made in the first night, and which thou didst hold truly. All the gain didst thou give me as a true man should. The other feint I proffered thee for the morrow: my fair wife kissed thee, and thou didst give me her kisses--for both those days I gave thee two blows without scathe--true man, true return. But the third time thou didst fail, and therefore hadst thou that blow. For 'tis my weed thou wearest, that same woven girdle, my own wife wrought it, that do I wot for sooth. Now know I well thy kisses, and thy conversation, and the wooing of my wife, for 'twas mine own doing. I sent her to try thee, and in sooth I think thou art the most faultless knight that ever trode earth. As a pearl among white peas is of more worth than they, so is Gawain, i' faith, by other knights. But thou didst lack a little, Sir Knight, and wast wanting in loyalty, yet that was for no evil work, nor for wooing neither, but because thou lovedst thy life--therefore I blame thee the less."

Then the other stood a great while, still sorely angered and vexed within himself; all the blood flew to his face, and he shrank for shame as the Green Knight spake; and the first words he said were, "Cursed be ye, cowardice and covetousness, for in ye is the destruction of virtue." Then he loosed the girdle, and gave it to the knight. "Lo, take there the falsity, may foul befall it! For fear of thy blow cowardice bade me make friends with covetousness and forsake the customs of largess and loyalty, which befit all knights. Now am I faulty and false and have been afeared: from treachery and untruth come sorrow and care. I avow to thee, Sir Knight, that I have ill done; do then thy will. I shall be more wary hereafter."

Then the other laughed and said gaily, "I wot I am whole of the hurt I had, and thou hast made such free confession of thy misdeeds, and hast so borne the penance of mine axe edge, that I hold thee absolved from that sin, and purged as clean as if thou hadst never sinned since thou wast born. And this girdle that is wrought with gold and green, like my raiment, do I give thee, Sir Gawain, that thou mayest think upon this chance when thou goest forth among princes of renown, and keep this for a token of the adventure of the Green Chapel, as it chanced between chivalrous knights. And thou shalt come again with me to my dwelling and pass the rest of this feast in gladness." Then the lord laid hold of him, and said, "I wot we shall soon make peace with my wife, who was thy bitter enemy."

"Nay, forsooth," said Sir Gawain, and seized his helmet and took it off swiftly, and thanked the knight: "I have fared ill, may bliss betide thee, and may He who rules all things reward thee swiftly. Commend me to that courteous lady, thy fair wife, and to the other my honoured ladies, who have beguiled their knight with skilful craft. But 'tis no marvel if one be made a fool and brought to sorrow by women's wiles, for so was Adam beguiled by one, and Solomon by many, and Samson all too soon, for Delilah dealt him his doom; and David thereafter was wedded with Bathsheba, which brought him much sorrow--if one might love a woman and believe her not, 'twere great gain! And since all they were beguiled by women, methinks 'tis the less blame to me that I was misled! But as for thy girdle, that will I take with good will, not for gain of the gold, nor for samite, nor silk, nor the costly pendants, neither for weal nor for worship, but in sign of my frailty. I shall look upon it when I ride in renown and remind myself of the fault and faintness of the flesh; and so when pride uplifts me for prowess of arms, the sight of this lace shall humble my heart. But one thing would I pray, if it displease thee not: since thou art lord of yonder land wherein I have dwelt, tell me what thy rightful name may be, and I will ask no more."

"That will I truly," quoth the other. "Bernlak de Hautdesert am I called in this land. Morgain le Fay dwelleth in mine house (12), and through knowledge of clerkly craft hath she taken many. For long time was she the mistress of Merlin, who knew well all you knights of the court. Morgain the goddess is she called therefore, and there is none so haughty but she can bring him low. She sent me in this guise to yon fair hall to test the truth of the renown that is spread abroad of the valour of the Round Table. She taught me this marvel to betray your wits, to vex Guinevere and fright her to death by the man who spake with his head in his hand at the high table. That is she who is at home, that ancient lady, she is even thine aunt, Arthur's half-sister, the daughter of the Duchess of Tintagel, who afterward married King Uther. Therefore I bid thee, knight, come to thine aunt, and make merry in thine house; my folk love thee, and I wish thee as well as any man on earth, by my faith, for thy true dealing."

But Sir Gawain said nay, he would in no wise do so; so they embraced and kissed, and commended each other to the Prince of Paradise, and parted right there, on the cold ground. Gawain on his steed rode swiftly to the king's hall, and the Green Knight got him whithersoever he would.

Sir Gawain who had thus won grace of his life, rode through wild ways on Gringalet; oft he lodged in a house, and oft without, and many adventures did he have and came off victor full often, as at this time I cannot relate in tale. The hurt that he had in his neck was healed, he bare the shining girdle as a baldric bound by his side, and made fast with a knot 'neath his left arm, in token that he was taken in a fault--and thus he came in safety again to the court.

Then joy awakened in that dwelling when the king knew that the good Sir Gawain was come, for he deemed it gain. King Arthur kissed the knight, and the queen also, and many valiant knights sought to embrace him. They asked him how he had fared, and he told them all that had chanced to him--the adventure of the chapel, the fashion of the knight, the love of the lady--at last of the lace. He showed them the wound in the neck which he won for his disloyalty at the hand of the knight, the blood flew to his face for shame as he told the tale.

"Lo, lady," he quoth, and handled the lace, "this is the bond of the blame that I bear in my neck, this is the harm and the loss I have suffered, the cowardice and covetousness in which I was caught, the token of my covenant in which I was taken. And I must needs wear it so long as I live, for none may hide his harm, but undone it may not be, for if it hath clung to thee once, it may never be severed."

Then the king comforted the knight, and the court laughed loudly at the tale, and all made accord that the lords and the ladies who belonged to the Round Table, each hero among them, should wear bound about him a baldric of bright green for the sake of Sir Gawain. (13) And to this was agreed all the honour of the Round Table, and he who ware it was honoured the more thereafter, as it is testified in the best book of romance. That in Arthur's days this adventure befell, the book of Brutus bears witness. For since that bold knight came hither first, and the siege and the assault were ceased at Troy, I wis

Many a venture herebefore
Hath fallen such as this:
May He that bare the crown of thorn
Bring us unto His bliss.

Amen.

NOTES

1. "The Legend of Sir Gawain," Grimm Library, Vol. VII. (Chapter IX. Sir Gawain and the Green Knight).

2. Dance accompanied by song. Often mentioned in old romances.

3. Agravain, "à la dure main." This characterisation of Gawain's brother seems to indicate that there was a French source at the root of this story. The author distinctly tells us more than once that the tale, as he tells it, was written in a book, M. Gaston Paris thinks that the direct source was an Anglo-Norman poem, now lost.

4. If any in this hall holds himself so hardy. This, the main incident of the tale, is apparently of very early date. The oldest version we possess is that found in the Irish tale of the Fled Bricrend (Bricriu's feast) [edited and translated by the Rev. G. Henderson, M.A., Irish Texts Society, vol. ii.], where the hero of the tale is the Irish champion, Cuchulinn. Two mediæval romances, the Mule sans Frein (French) and Diu Krône (German), again attribute it to Gawain; while the continuator of Chrétien de Troye's Conte del Graal gives as hero a certain Carados, whom he represents as Arthur's nephew; and the prose Perceval has Lancelot. So far as the mediæval versions are concerned, the original hero is undoubtedly Gawain; and our poem gives the fullest and most complete form of the story we possess. In the Irish version the magician is a giant, and the abnormal size and stature of the Green Knight is, in all probability, the survival of a primitive feature. His curious colour is a trait found nowhere else. In Diu Krône we are told that the challenger changes shapes in a terrifying manner, but no details are given.

5. For Yule was over-past. This passage, descriptive of the flight of the year, should be especially noticed. Combined with the other passages--the description of Gawain's journey, the early morning hunts, the dawning of New Year's Day, and the ride to the Green Chapel--they indicate a knowledge of Nature, and an observant eye

for her moods, uncommon among mediæval poets. It is usual enough to find graceful and charming descriptions of spring and early summer--an appreciation of May in especial, when the summer courts were held, is part of the stock-in-trade of mediæval romancers--but a sympathy with the year in all its changes is far rarer, and certainly deserves to be specially reckoned to the credit of this nameless writer.

6. First a rich carpet was stretched on the floor. The description of the arming of Gawain is rather more detailed in the original, but some of the minor points are not easy to understand, the identification of sundry of the pieces of armour being doubtful.

7. The pentangle painted thereupon in gleaming gold. I do not remember that the pentangle is elsewhere attributed to Gawain. He often bears a red shield; but the blazon varies. Indeed, the heraldic devices borne by Arthur's knights are distractingly chaotic--their legends are older than the science of heraldry, and no one has done for them the good office that the compiler of the Thidrek Saga has rendered to his Teutonic heroes.

8. The Wilderness of Wirral. This is in Cheshire. Sir F. Madden suggests that the forest which forms the final stage of Gawain's journey is that of Inglewood, in Cumberland. The geography here is far clearer than is often the case in such descriptions.

9. 'Twas the fairest castle that ever a knight owned. Here, again, I have omitted some of the details of the original, the architectural terms lacking identification.

10. With blast of the bugle fared forth to the field. The account of each day's hunting contains a number of obsolete terms and details of woodcraft, not given in full. The meaning of some has been lost, and the minute descriptions of skinning and dismembering the game would be distinctly repulsive to the general reader. They are valuable for a student of the history of the English sport, but interfere with the progress of the story. The fact that the author devotes so much space to them seems to indicate that he lived in the country and was keenly interested in field sports. (Gottfried von Strassbourg's Tristan contains a similar and almost more detailed description.)

11. I will give [you] my girdle. This magic girdle, which confers invulnerability on its owner, is a noticeable feature of our story. It is found nowhere else in this connection, yet in other romances we find that Gawain possesses a girdle with similar powers (cf., my Legend of Sir Gawain, Chap. IX.). Such a talisman was also owned by Cuchulinn, the Irish hero, who has many points of contact with Gawain. It seems not

improbable that this was also an old feature of the story. I have commented, in the Introduction, on the lady's persistent wooing of Gawain, and need not repeat the remarks here. The Celtic Lay of the Great Fool (Amadan Mor) presents some curious points of contact with our story, which may, however, well be noted here. In the Lay the hero is mysteriously deprived of his legs, through the draught from a cup proffered by a Gruagach or magician. He comes to a castle, the lord of which goes out hunting, leaving his wife in the care of the Great Fool, who is to allow no man to enter. He falls asleep, and a young knight arrives and kisses the host's wife. The Great Fool, awaking, refuses to allow the intruder to depart; and, in spite of threats and blandishments, insists on detaining him till the husband returns. Finally, the stranger reveals himself as the host in another shape; he is also the Gruagach, who deprived the hero of his limbs, and the Great Fool's brother. He has only intended to test the Amadon Mor's fidelity. A curious point in connection with this story is that it possesses a prose opening which shows a marked affinity with the "Perceval" enfances. That the Perceval and Gawain stories early became connected is certain, but what is the precise connection between them and the Celtic Lay is not clear. In its present form the latter is certainly posterior to the Grail romances, but it is quite possible that the matter with which it deals represents a tradition older than the Arthurian story.

12. *Morgain le Fay, who dwelleth in my house.* The enmity between Morgain le Fay and Guinevere, which is here stated to have been the motif of the enchantment, is no invention of the author, but is found in the Merlin, probably the earliest of the Arthurian prose romances. In a later version of our story, a poem, written in ballad form, and contained in the "Percy" MS., Morgain does not appear; her place is taken by an old witch, mother to the lady, but the enchantment is still due to her spells. In this later form the knight bears the curious name of Sir Bredbeddle. That given in our romance, Bernlak de Hautdesert,, seems to point to the original French source of the story. (It is curious that Morgain should here be represented as extremely old, while Arthur is still in his first youth. There is evidently a discrepancy or misunderstanding of the source here.)

13. *A baldric of bright green, for sake of Sir Gawain.* The later version connects this lace with that worn by the knights of the Bath; but this latter was white, not green. The knights wore it on the left shoulder till they had done some gallant deed, or till some noble lady took it off for them.

Sir Gawain and the Green Knight, The Lady of Shallot, The Lady of the Fountain, and other Classic Poems and Tales of Camelot

The Lady of Shalott

Alfred, Lord Tennyson (1833)

Part I

On either side the river lie
Long fields of barley and of rye,
That clothe the wold and meet the sky;
And thro' the field the road runs by
   To many-tower'd Camelot;
And up and down the people go,
Gazing where the lilies blow
Round an island there below,
   The island of Shalott.

Willows whiten, aspens quiver,
Little breezes dusk and shiver
Thro' the wave that runs for ever
By the island in the river
   Flowing down to Camelot.
Four gray walls, and four gray towers,
Overlook a space of flowers,
And the silent isle imbowers
   The Lady of Shalott.

By the margin, willow veil'd,
Slide the heavy barges trail'd
By slow horses; and unhail'd
The shallop flitteth silken-sail'd
   Skimming down to Camelot:
But who hath seen her wave her hand?
Or at the casement seen her stand?
Or is she known in all the land,
   The Lady of Shalott?

Only reapers, reaping early
In among the bearded barley,
Hear a song that echoes cheerly
From the river winding clearly,
   Down to tower'd Camelot:
And by the moon the reaper weary,
Piling sheaves in uplands airy,
Listening, whispers " 'Tis the fairy
   Lady of Shalott."

Part II

There she weaves by night and day
A magic web with colours gay.
She has heard a whisper say,
A curse is on her if she stay
   To look down to Camelot.
She knows not what the curse may be,
And so she weaveth steadily,
And little other care hath she,
   The Lady of Shalott.

And moving thro' a mirror clear
That hangs before her all the year,
Shadows of the world appear.
There she sees the highway near
   Winding down to Camelot:
There the river eddy whirls,
And there the surly village-churls,
And the red cloaks of market girls,
   Pass onward from Shalott.

Sometimes a troop of damsels glad,
An abbot on an ambling pad,
Sometimes a curly shepherd-lad,
Or long-hair'd page in crimson clad,
 Goes by to tower'd Camelot;
And sometimes thro' the mirror blue
The knights come riding two and two:
She hath no loyal knight and true,
 The Lady of Shalott.

But in her web she still delights
To weave the mirror's magic sights,
For often thro' the silent nights
A funeral, with plumes and lights
 And music, went to Camelot:
Or when the moon was overhead,
Came two young lovers lately wed:
"I am half sick of shadows," said
 The Lady of Shalott.

Part III

A bow-shot from her bower-eaves,
He rode between the barley-sheaves,
The sun came dazzling thro' the leaves,
And flamed upon the brazen greaves
 Of bold Sir Lancelot.
A red-cross knight for ever kneel'd
To a lady in his shield,
That sparkled on the yellow field,
 Beside remote Shalott.

All in the blue unclouded weather
Thick-jewell'd shone the saddle-leather,
The helmet and the helmet-feather
Burn'd like one burning flame together,
 As he rode down to Camelot.
As often thro' the purple night,
Below the starry clusters bright,
Some bearded meteor, trailing light,
 Moves over still Shalott.

His broad clear brow in sunlight glow'd;
On burnish'd hooves his war-horse trode;
From underneath his helmet flow'd
His coal-black curls as on he rode,
 As he rode down to Camelot.
From the bank and from the river
He flash'd into the crystal mirror,
"Tirra lirra," by the river
 Sang Sir Lancelot.

She left the web, she left the loom,
She made three paces thro' the room,
She saw the water-lily bloom,
She saw the helmet and the plume,
 She look'd down to Camelot.
Out flew the web and floated wide;
The mirror crack'd from side to side;
"The curse is come upon me," cried
 The Lady of Shalott.

Part IV

In the stormy east-wind straining,
The pale yellow woods were waning,
The broad stream in his banks complaining,
Heavily the low sky raining
   Over tower'd Camelot;
Down she came and found a boat
Beneath a willow left afloat,
And round about the prow she wrote
   The Lady of Shalott.

And down the river's dim expanse
Like some bold seer in a trance,
Seeing all his own mischance--
With a glassy countenance
   Did she look to Camelot.
And at the closing of the day
She loosed the chain, and down she lay;
The broad stream bore her far away,
   The Lady of Shalott.

Lying, robed in snowy white
That loosely flew to left and right--
The leaves upon her falling light--
Thro' the noises of the night
   She floated down to Camelot:
And as the boat-head wound along
The willowy hills and fields among,
They heard her singing her last song,
   The Lady of Shalott.

Heard a carol, mournful, holy,
Chanted loudly, chanted lowly,
Till her blood was frozen slowly,
And her eyes were darken'd wholly,
   Turn'd to tower'd Camelot.
For ere she reach'd upon the tide
The first house by the water-side,
Singing in her song she died,
   The Lady of Shalott.

Under tower and balcony,
By garden-wall and gallery,
A gleaming shape she floated by,
Dead-pale between the houses high,
   Silent into Camelot.
Out upon the wharfs they came,
Knight and burgher, lord and dame,
And round the prow they read her name,
   The Lady of Shalott.

Who is this? and what is here?
And in the lighted palace near
Died the sound of royal cheer;
And they cross'd themselves for fear,
   All the knights at Camelot:
But Lancelot mused a little space;
He said, "She has a lovely face;
God in his mercy lend her grace,
   The Lady of Shalott."

Sir Gawain and the Green Knight, The Lady of Shallot, The Lady of the Fountain, and other Classic Poems and Tales of Camelot

The Founding of the Round Table

Layamon - Translation: Jessie L. Weston (1914)

IT chanced on a Yule-tide day
That King Arthur in London lay;
There had come to him at that tide
Vassals from far and wide;
From Scotland, and Britain bold,
From Ireland, and Iceland cold,
From every folk and land
That had bowed them to Arthur's hand.

They had sent their highest thanes,
With their horses and serving swains:
And beside the folk that, still,
Bowed them to Arthur's will,
Came seven kings' sons, I ween,
With seven hundred knights so keen.

Now each man thought in his heart
That to him fell the higher part,
And each man deemed that he were
Better than this, his peer;
The folk came from diverse lands
And envy came with their bands --
This one held him of high degree,
This other, much higher than he!

Then they blew the trumpets' blast,
And they set the boards full fast,
And bare water to young and old
In basons of good red gold.

Soft were the cloths in the hall,
Of white silk woven all.
There Arthur sat in his pride,
With Wenhavere, the queen, at his side,
And the guests in order right,
First earl, then baron, then knight,
Each found his appointed seat
As the king's men deemed it meet.

There were men right nobly born
Who did service that Yule-tide morn,
And bare the meat forth-right
To each gay and gallant knight.
Then they turned them toward the thanes,
And below those still, the swains,
Thus served they, one and all,
The folk in King Arthur's hall.

Thus all for a space went well --
But after, a change befell,
For the folk, they fell to strife,
And blows were among them rife.

First they threw the loaves of bread,
And then, when the last was sped,
The bowls of silver-shine
Filled with the good red wine.

Thereafter with fists they fought
Each the neck of his foeman sought.

Then sprang forth a young man there, --
(From Winet land did he fare
As hostage to Arthur's hand,
The king's son of Winet land,
Rumaret was his father hight --)
And out spake that gallant knight,
And cried on the king that hour;
"Lord Arthur, get to thy bower,
And take with thee Wenhavere,
And the kinsmen thou holdest dear,
And we shall fight out this fray
With the foreign folk to-day!"

And e'en as he spake the word
He leapt to the royal board
Where lay the sharp knives keen,
For the service of king and queen;
Three knives he grasped in his hand,
And he smote the chief of the band
And clave the neck of the knight
Who first began the fight,
With a blow so swift and sore
That his head rolled e'en to the floor.

Thereafter he slew another,
Even that first thane's brother,
Ere the swords might come to the hall
Seven men had he slain in all.
'Twas a grim and a grisly fight,
Each man would the other smite,
Blood gushed forth at every stroke,
Bale was upon the folk.

Then forth from the king's bower strode
Arthur in wrathful mood,
And with him a hundred knights
In helmet and burnie bright;
Each bare in his strong right hand
A gleaming white steel brand.

Then Arthur, king most dear,
Cried so that all might hear:
"Sit ye down, sit ye down, each one,
As ye love your lives, sit down!
He that will not while yet he may
I doom him to death straightway!
Now take me that self-same man
Who first this fight began;
Round his neck put a withy stout,
And draw him the hall without
To the moorland and marsh hard by;
There shall ye let him lie!

Then seek out his next of kin,
All such as be here within,
And with your broad swords keen
Shall ye strike off their heads, I ween!

Then take ye his women-folk,
And with swift, and with cunning, stroke
Carve off their noses there
That they be no longer fair.

And thus will I bring to shame
The kindred of which he came!
And if it be brought to my ear,
Or I otherwise chance to hear,
That one of my house or hold,
High or low, or young or old,
Shall hereafter awaken strife
For this slaughter, I swear on my life,
Neither gold, nor goodly steed,
Nor treasure, nor warlike weed
Shall be ransom for that man's head
That he be not swiftly dead,
Or horses his limbs shall draw --
So speak I the traitor's law!

*Sir Gawain and the Green Knight, The Lady of Shallot, The Lady of the Fountain,
and other Classic Poems and Tales of Camelot*

Bring me the hallows here,
On them will I soothly swear,
And so shall ye too, my knights,
And all who were at this fight."

First Arthur, the noblest of kings,
He swore by the holy things;
Then earls, and barons, and thanes,
And last of them all, the swains,
A solemn oath they swore
To wake that strife never more.

Then the dead men, one and all,
They bare them from out the hall,
And laid them low in the earth --
Then the trumpets they blew with mirth.

Each of them, were he lief or loth,
Must needs take water and cloth,
And they sat them, at one accord
Once more, adown to the board,
For they feared King Arthur's hand,
Noblest of kings on land

The cupbearers went their round,
The harpers made merry sound,
The glee-men sang songs so good,
The folk were in gladsome mood;
Thus for full seven days all told
King Arthur his feast did hold.

Thereafter I'ld have ye know,
To Cornwall the king would go,
And there cometh to him anon
A crafty and skilful man,
And he met the king in the way,
And in greeting fair did say:
"Arthur, all hail to thee now!

Noblest of kings art thou,
I am thine own true man,
To serve thee as well I can.
I have journeyed in many a land,
Right skilful is this, mine hand,
In craft of wood, or of tree, --
But now it was told to me
The slaughter thy knights had wrought,
When of late at thy board they fought,
And how, on mid-winter's day,
Mickle pride wrought murderous play;
For that each man by right of kin,
And high lineage, would sit within.

Now I will for thee, lord, prepare
A board exceeding fair,
Where sixteen hundred may sit,
And more, if it seem thee fit.

And all they shall turn about,
So that no man shall be without,
But without and within shall they be,
Man against man, verily!

And when thou to ride art fain,
Thou shalt carry it in thy train;
And when thou shalt hold thee still,
Thou shalt stablish it at thy will;
And never shalt thou fear more,
So long as the world endure,
That for envy a moody knight
Shall raise at thy board a fight,
Of high or of low degree
All men there shall equal be!"

Then they bade men timber win
That he might the board begin;
For the space of four weeks he wrought
Ere the work to an end he brought.

Then when a high day was come
The folk he called, every one;
And Arthur himself, the lord,
Sat him down at the new-wrought board,
And he bade every gallant knight
Take his place at his side forth-right,
And when each had found his seat,
And all were sat down to meat,
Then each man spake with the other
In such wise as he were his brother.

In order they sat about,
And no man was left without;
No knight, whatsoe'er his race,
But found there a fitting place,
Were he high, were he low, in that hall
Was a place for each and all.

And each man, he quaffed at the board
The drink that was there outpoured,
Nor thought he might call for other
Than the draught that would serve his brother.

Now this was that very Round Table
Of which Britons oft-times fable;
And many a lie shall ye hear
Of Arthur that king so dear;
But I think me 't is ever so
That the custom of men doth go,
He that loveth his friend, I ween,
For his honour is over-keen,
Nor shall deem it a shame to lie
If he win him more praise thereby!

The songs that the songmen sing
Of Arthur, the noble king,
All lies are they not, nor all sooth,
But this do I hold for the truth,
There was never such other lord
So mighty in deed and in word,
For so ye may find it writ
In his history, every whit,
From the first to the last, how things
Fell out for Arthur, the king.

Neither more nor less may ye read,
But all these, his acts, and his deeds.
The Britons, they loved him well,
And many a tale they tell,
And many a wondrous thing
Concerning Arthur, the king,
Such as never were wrought by man
Since ever the world began!

Yet he who would speak but the truth
He may find, in very sooth,
Enough to shape goodly rhymes
Of Arthur, the king, and his times.

Sir Gawain and the Green Knight, The Lady of Shallot, The Lady of the Fountain,
and other Classic Poems and Tales of Camelot

The Passing of Arthur

Layamon - Translation: Jessie L. Weston (1914)

A-HORSE to the king's host drew
A knight, both good and true,
Tidings he thought to bring
To Arthur, the Britons' king,
Of Modred his sister's son --
A welcome glad he won
From the king, who thought to hear
That which should bring him cheer.
Arthur lay long that night
And spake with that youthful knight,
But never a word did he say
Of that which had chanced alway.

When it came to the morrow's morn,
And the folk, they stirred with the dawn,
Then Arthur arose from his bed;
He stretched his arms over his head,
Then he stood, and he sat again,
E'en as one for misease is fain.
Then asked him that goodly knight,
"Lord, how hast thou passed the night?"

And Arthur, the king so good,
Made answer in troubled mood:
"Last night, as I lay on sleep
In my tent, and slumbered deep,
There came such a dream to me
As hath vexed me right bitterly --
Methought men lifted me there,
And raised me high in air,
Until that the roof-tree tall
I bestrode, of a lofty hall,
I sat there as I would ride, --

And below me, stretched out wide,
I saw all my goodly land;
Before me, sword in hand,
Sat Walwain, my kinsman true.

Then Modred towards us drew,
With him came a goodly throng;
In his hand was an axe so strong
And with mighty strokes he felled
The posts that the hall upheld.

And then I saw Wenhavere,
(Woman to me most dear,)
With her hands the roof she tare
Of that hall, so great and fair,
Till the building rocked and swayed,
And I fell to the ground dismayed;
And there my right arm I brake --
'Take that!' so Modred spake.

Then in ruins fell that hall,
And it bare Walwain in its fall
From the roof-tree e'en to the ground,
And he brake both arms at that stound.

Then I gripped my sword so good
In my left hand, as best I could,
And smote off Modred's head,
On the wold he fell down dead.

In pieces I hewed the queen
With my sword blade, good and keen,
And, methought, her corse at last
In a deep black pit I cast.

51

Sir Gawain and the Green Knight, The Lady of Shallot, The Lady of the Fountain,
and other Classic Poems and Tales of Camelot

My folk, they had fled away,
And I knew not, by Christ, that day
Whither they all had gone --
But methought I stood alone
On a moor-land bleak and cold;
I wandered afar on the wold,
Gryphons I saw, I trow,
And grisley fowls enow!

Then over the down to me
Came a beast, most fair to see,
A golden lion, methought
'T was a work that God's hand had wrought!

The beast came to me forthright,
By the middle it gripped me tight,
And carried me o'er the land
Till we came to the salt sea strand,
And I saw the waves of the sea
How they drave right heavily.
Then the lion the flood would swim,
Bearing me ever with him,
But scarce were we come in the sea
Ere the waves bare him far from me.

Then a great fish came in my need,
And bare me to land with speed;
I was wet and weary, I trow,
For sorrow, and sick enow!

And then must I needs awake,
My heart did within me quake.
Then a heat and a trembling fell,
And I burned as with fires of Hell!

Thus all night long have I lain
And dreamed that dream o'er again,
'T is a token true, I wis,
That vanished is all my bliss,
And, while life be left to me,
Grief shall my portion be!

Alas! that I have not here
Wenhavere my queen so dear."
Then out spake that youthful knight:
"My lord, thou doest not right,
No man should so read a dream
As to turn it to sorrow, I ween!

For of all kings, I know full well,
Who under the welkin dwell,
To whose rule the people bow,
The richest and wisest art thou!

And if it should chance to be,
(May Christ keep it far from thee!)
That Modred, thy sister's son,
The heart of thy queen had won,
And had taken thy wife and thy land,
And had set them all in his hand,
(All thou didst leave in his care
When thou thoughtest afar to fare,)
And were thus for a traitor shown, --
Still mightest thou hold thine own,
And avenge thyself by war,
And rule thy folk as before,
And the men who this wrong had done
Thou could'st slay them every one,
Yea, and sweep them clean from the ground,
So that none should alive be found!"

Sir Gawain and the Green Knight, The Lady of Shallot, The Lady of the Fountain, and other Classic Poems and Tales of Camelot

Arthur, he answered then:
(Noblest was he of men,)
"So long as 'ever' may be
Ne'er do I think to see
The day that my kinsman dear,
The man to my heart most near,
Hath ever such treason planned
As to seize my crown and my land;
Or Wenhavere, my queen and love,
Shall other than steadfast prove!

Such work they would ne'er begin,
Tho' they thought thus the world to win!"

As he spake the word, forthright
There answered that gallant knight:
"I speak but the truth, my King,
For I am thine underling,
Even thus hath Modred done,
The heart of thy queen hath he won,
And all Britain, and thy fair land,
Hath he taken in his own hand.

As king and queen do they reign
Nor deem thou shalt come again,
'T is a far cry to the Roman shore,
From thence shalt thou come no more!
But I am thy man O King!

And I saw this evil thing,
To thyself have I brought this word,
And the truth, e'en as thou hast heard,
My head in pledge will I lay,
'T is sooth and no lie, that I say,
But even thus have they done,
Thy queen and thy sister's son,
Modred hath taken thy throne,
Thy land, and thy wife, for his own!"

Then never man stirred of all
Those knights in King Arthur's hall,
Right sorrowful was their mood
For the grief of their king so good.
Downcast and sad of mien
Were the British men, I ween!

'T was thus for a space, and then
Rose a clamour of angry men,
Till all far and wide might know
Of the Britons' wrath and woe!

In sooth might ye there have heard
Full many a threatening word,
Doom to the faithless pair,
Modred and the queen, they sware,
And the men who held with the twain
They all should be swiftly slain.

Then Arthur cried thro' the hall,
Fairest of Britons all,
"Sit ye down, and hold ye still
My knights, and hearken my will,
Strange words do I think to say,
To-morrow, when it be day,
By Christ, His power, and His grace,
Will I get me forth from this place.

To Britain I take my way,
And there will I Modred slay,
And the queen with fire will I burn;
And to loss and to ruin turn
All that have joined their hand
With them, and this treason planned.

But here will I leave in my place
Hoel, the fair of face,
(The first of my kinsmen he,
And dearest of men to me,)

Sir Gawain and the Green Knight, The Lady of Shallot, The Lady of the Fountain, and other Classic Poems and Tales of Camelot

With half of my army bold
That this kingdom he keep and hold,
And all this goodly land
That I late have set in mine hand.

And when I have vengeance ta'en
I will turn me to Rome again,
And my lands so wide and fair
Will I give into Walwain's care.
No empty threat do I make
But my life on my word I stake,
I will fell my foes every one,
Who this treason and wrong have done!"

Then Walwain arose in the ring,
He was kinsman unto the king,
Wrathful and stern his mood,
And he spake, "O almighty God,
Who dost judgment and doom award,
And this middle earth dost guard,
How did this thing begin?
Why hath Modred wrought this sin?

Now ye folk, lend to me the ear;
This day I forsake him here,
I myself will his Doomsman be,
(So the Lord grant it unto me!)
Higher than e'er another
With this hand will I hang my brother!
And the queen I will judge by God's law,
Wild horses her limbs shall draw.

For never shall I be blithe
The while that I be alive
Till I right mine uncle and lord
To the best of my hand and sword!"

The Britons made answer then
With one voice, as valiant men:
"Our weapons are keen and bright,
To-morrow we march forthright!"

Then, since the Lord willed it so,
To-morrow they forth would go,
Arthur moved with the dawning light,
And with him his valiant knights,
One half of the folk must stay,
And one half marched with him alway.

Thus he led his men through the land
Till they came at the last to Whitsand;
Ships, full many and good,
Ready in harbour stood,
But a fortnight full his host
It lay becalmed on that coast,
Till the weather changed once more,
And the wind blew fresh from the shore.

Now in Arthur's host that day
Was one who would traitor play,
And when he heard men speak
Of the vengeance they thought to wreak,
Forthwith he took his swain,
And he bade him haste amain,

And bear to Wenhavere the word
Of how Arthur the tale had heard,
And how he would come ere long,
With a mickle host, and strong;
And how he had sworn an oath
To take vengeance upon them both.

Sir Gawain and the Green Knight, The Lady of Shallot, The Lady of the Fountain,
and other Classic Poems and Tales of Camelot

The queen came to Modred then,
(Dearest to her of men,)
And told to him everything
Concerning Arthur the king,
How he would act in that day,
And how he the twain would slay.

Then Modred sent speedily
To Saxland across the sea,
And he prayed that Childerich,
A monarch exceeding rich,
Would swiftly to Britain fare,
(Of the land should he have his share --)
And he prayed of the king that tide
To send messengers far and wide,
East, West, and South, and North,
And bid all his knights fare forth,
Even all they met on their way, --
And to get them without delay
To Britain, and part of the land
Would he give into Childerich's hand;
North of the Humber all
Should be his without recall,
If he men to his aid would bring
Against Arthur his lord and king.

Childerich helped him in need,
To Britain he came with speed;
And Modred called on his men
To gather for battle then,
There were sixty thousand all told,
Hardy warriors and bold,
Who were come out of Heathennesse
For King Arthur's sore distress,
For Modred they came to fight,
That evil and traitorous knight!

And when all were come to the place,
Of every folk and race,
Rank upon rank did they press,
One hundred thousand, no less,
Of heathen, or Christian, that morn
Were with Modred the false and
foresworn.

Now Arthur and all his host,
At Whitsand they lay, on the coast,
Too long seemed those fourteen days --
And Modred he knew always
What Arthur he planned and he wrought,
For tidings each day were brought
From the army that lay by the sea --
Then the rain, it rained steadily,
And the wind, it shifted at last,
And blew from the east full blast,
And Arthur gat him aboard
With every knight and lord;
And he bade his shipmen steer
For Romney, and have no fear,
There he thought him to land, and then
March inland with all his men.

When they came to the haven and shore
Modred was there before,
And ere ever the dawn grew bright
The hosts they had fallen to fight,
And they fought through the live-long day,
Full many there lifeless lay!

Some of them fought on the land,
And some on the salt sea strand,
Some from the ships' deck cast
Sharp spears, which flew full fast.

55

Walwain, he went before,
And cleared their path to the shore,
Eleven thanes did he slay
With Childerich's son, that day,
Whom his father had hither brought --
When the sun his rest had sought
Bowed was each British head
For Walwain lay there dead
And robbed of his life-days all --
(Through a Saxon earl did he fall,
Sorry be that man's soul!)

To Arthur 't was bitter dole,
Full sorrowful was his mood,
And he spake, that chieftain good,
(Mightiest of Britons he --)
"I have lost, ah, woe is me!

Walwain whom I loved so well,
E'en so did my dream foretell,
I deemed it would sorrow bring!

Now slain is Angel the king,
Who was mine own darling, and thane,
And my sister's son, Walwain,
Ah, woe is me for this morn,
I would I had ne'er been born!

Now up from your ships, and fight
As ye ne'er yet have fought, my knights!"

Then, even at his command,
His warriors leapt to the land,
Sixty thousand all told,
Stalwart Britons and bold,
And they brake through Modred's host,
Well nigh he himself was lost!

Then Modred, he 'gan to flee
And his men followed speedily,
'T was a marvel to see how they fled,
The fields rocked beneath their tread,
And the stones in the river course
Jarred 'neath the blood-streams' force!

Full well had they ended that fight
Were it not for the coming of night,
Had the darkness but made delay
All their foes had been slain that day.

The night fell between the twain --
O'er the hills Modred fled amain,
He fled so far and so fast
That to London he came at last,
But they knew, the burghers stout,
How the matter had fallen out,
And bade him and his followers all
Abide there, without the wall.

Modred, he might not stay,
But to Winchester took his way,
And they gave him shelter there
And all that with him did fare.

But Arthur, with all his might,
Pursued after him forth-right,
And to Winchester came ere long
With a mickle host and strong;
With his army he sat him down,
And shut Modred within the town.

When Modred saw him so nigh
He bethought him craftily,
And oft he turned in his mind
What counsel he there might find.

Sir Gawain and the Green Knight, The Lady of Shallot, The Lady of the Fountain, and other Classic Poems and Tales of Camelot

And there, on that self-same night,
He called unto him his knights,
And bade them to arm them straight
And march out of the city gate,
For there would he make a stand
And fight for the crown and the land.

And unto the burghers he swore
Free law for evermore
Would they stand by him at his need
And help him with act and deed.

And thus, when it waxed to light,
All ordered they stood for fight.
Arthur beheld this thing,
Wroth was the Britons' king:
Then the trumpet blast rang clear,
And his men came together there,
And he prayed of his thanes forth-right,
And of every noble knight,
To help him, and fight right well,
That he might all his foemen fell;
And to level the city wall,
And to hang the burghers all.

Together they marched, as one man,
And sternly the fight began.
Then Modred, again he thought
In his heart, and counsel sought,
And he did in his danger there
E'en as he did elsewhere,
With the best could he traitor play
For treason he wrought alway!

He worked a betrayal grim
On the comrades who fought for him;
For he called from among the rest
The knights whom he loved the best,
And the friends whom he held most dear
Of the folk who were with him there,
And he stole from the fight away --
The Devil led him that day!

And left his good folk on the land,
To be slain there by Arthur's hand.
Thus all day long they fought,
That their lord was nigh they thought,
And they deemed that he took good heed
To succour them in their need.

But Modred, he went his way
On the road that toward Hampton lay,
And made for the haven then --
(Wickedest he of men! --)
Of the ships he took speedily
All that were fitted for sea,
And the steersmen, one and all,
That no harm should his ships befall;
Thus Modred, that traitorous king,
Did they safe into Cornwall bring.
And Arthur his army cast
Round Winchester, fair and fast,
And all the folk did he slay --
Sorrow was their's that day! --
He spared no soul that drew breath,
Young or old, all he put to death.

Thus the people to loss he turned,
And the city with fire he burned.
And then he bade them withal
To break down the city wall;
And thus was fulfilled the word,
Aforetime from Merlin heard:
"Winchester, woe unto thee,
For swallowed of earth shalt thou be!"

Sir Gawain and the Green Knight, The Lady of Shallot, The Lady of the Fountain, and other Classic Poems and Tales of Camelot

Thus Merlin the seer foretold,
Wisest wizard of old!
In York the queen abode,
Right sorrowful was her mood,
Saddest of women, I ween,
Was Wenhavere, Arthur's queen!

For she heard men say for sooth,
And knew them for words of truth,
How that Modred, he ever fled,
And Arthur behind him sped,
Woe was upon her that morn
That ever she had been born!

From York did she take her flight,
In secret, by shades of night,
And to Caerleon made her way
Swiftly, without delay,
Not for all this world's treasure-store
Would she look upon Arthur more.

Thus with but two knights in her train
At Caerleon she drew rein,
To the city she came by night,
And they hooded her there forth-right,
And a nun must she henceforth be,
Saddest of women she!

Then men of the queen knew naught,
Where she went, or what fate she sought;
E'en when many years had flown
The truth might by none be known.

And never a book may tell
In what wise her death befell,
And if in the water's flow
She cast herself, none may know.

In Cornwall was Modred then,
And he gathered to him his men;
To Ireland he sent with speed
Messengers in his need,
To Scotland, to Saxland, too,
Help from them all he drew.

He bade them come to his land,
All who would win to their hand
Silver, or gold, or fee --
Thus he guarded him prudently,
As a wise man will ever do
When need forceth him thereto.

Tidings to Arthur they bring,
(Was never so wroth a king!)
How Modred in Cornwall sped, --
That a mighty host he led,
And there he thought to abide
Till Arthur should 'gainst him ride.

Then messengers Arthur sent,
Through the breadth of his land they went,
And they bade every living knight
In the land, who had strength to fight,
To arm him, and come straightway. --
But if he would traitor play,
And hold with Modred, then
The king would have none of such men.

And when Modred the tidings knew
Toward him he swiftly drew --
Countless the folk that day,
O'er many of them were fey!

Sir Gawain and the Green Knight, The Lady of Shallot, The Lady of the Fountain, and other Classic Poems and Tales of Camelot

To the Tamar their face they set,
By the river those armies met,
Camelford, did they call that shore,
And the name dureth ever more!

Arthur, he reckoned then
On his side, sixty thousand men,
But more by thousands were they
Who stood by Modred that day!

No longer would Arthur abide
But thitherward would he ride;
Bold were his knights and fleet,
They hasted their fate to meet!

On the banks of the Tamar river
The armies they came together,
The banners above them flew,
The ranks together drew,

Their long swords flash in the light,
Hard on the helms they smite;
The sparks sprang beneath the stroke,
The spears, they shivered and broke;
Cloven each goodly shield,
The shafts they splinter and yield;
The folk they fought passing well,
Their number no man might tell;
Tamar, it ran on flood
Swollen with streams of blood.

Never might man in the fight
Know one from the other knight,
Who did better, or who did worse,
So mingled the battle's course,
For each, as he might, would slay,
Were he swain, were he knight, that day!

There was Modred of life-days reft,
On the field was he lifeless left,
And with him all of his knights
Were slain in that fearsome fight.

There too were slain, I ween,
Full many good knights and keen,
King Arthur's warriors brave
High and low, all found there their grave,
With every British lord
Who sat at Arthur's board,
And the men who bowed to his hand
Of every kin and land.

And Arthur was smitten sore,
Of spear wounds that day he bore
Fifteen, so deep, and so wide,
In the least gash two gloves might ye hide!

When it came to the end of the strife
Nor more were there left on life,
Of two hundred thousand men
Who lay hewn in pieces then,
Save only Arthur, the king,
And two knights of his following.
And Arthur was smitten sore,
Wondrous the wounds he bore!

Then a young knight came to the king,
He was one of his kith and kin, --
Son to Cador the keen,
Who earl of Cornwall had been,
Constantine was he hight,
Arthur he loved that knight --
The king looked his face toward
As he lay on the bloody sward,
And thus he spake to the lad
With sorrowful heart and sad:

Sir Gawain and the Green Knight, The Lady of Shallot, The Lady of the Fountain, and other Classic Poems and Tales of Camelot

"Constantine, thou art welcome now,
Cador's son wert thou,
I leave thee my kingdom here,
Guard thou my Britons dear
So long as thy life shall last --
And see that they still hold fast
The laws that in my day stood,
And King Uther's laws so good.

But to Avalon will I fare,
A maiden, she ruleth there,
By name Argante the queen,
Fairest of elves I ween!

My wounds shall she handle and heal,
Turning my woe to weal,
For sound is he who hath quaffed
At her hand a healing draught!

And then will I come again
And once more o'er my kingdom reign,
And dwell with my Britons dear
In great joy, and mickle cheer!"

And e'en as the words he said
Swift o'er the sea there sped
A little boat, and low,
That came with the wavelets' flow.

Within were two women fair
Who a wondrous semblance bare;
They took up Arthur the king,
And swift to the boat did bring,
Soft they laid down his head,
And swiftly from thence they sped.

Ah! then was fulfilled the word
From Merlin the prophet heard
That sorrow and woe should spring
From the passing of Arthur the king.

But the British folk, they say
That Arthur, he lives alway,
That held by a fairy spell,
In Avalon doth he dwell;
And each Briton's hope is strong
That he cometh again ere long!

And there liveth no mother's son
Who desire of women hath won,
Who knoweth a better lore
Or of Arthur can tell ye more.
But whilom was a wizard wight,
Merlin that man was hight,
And he said in words of truth,
(For ever his sayings were sooth,)
That Arthur shall come again,
And once more o'er the Britons reign!

Sir Gawain and the Green Knight, The Lady of Shallot, The Lady of the Fountain, and other Classic Poems and Tales of Camelot

The Morte D'arthur
Wilfrid Scawen Blunt (1914)

THESE are the tales in all their valorous lore

Of that famed frolic of the Table Round

No shame-faced verse, but stout prose to the core,

As Malory wrote it and our fathers found.

Tales touching still, and still through time renowned,

But less, methinks, for their high deeds that bore

Their crests so proudly than the one lost sound

Of Lancelot's step at the Queen's chamber door.

— How their sighs echo! Think, if then she had made

Another answer than her human "Yes,"

And been more valiant and denied and slept!

Should we still weep o'er Bors and Galahad,

The Sancgreal's quest, Gawayne in wrath equipped,

Or all King Arthur's jousts in Lyonnesse?

The Lady of the Fountain

Translated from Old English by Lady Charlotte Elizabeth Guest (1877)

King Arthur was at Caerlleon upon Usk; and one day he sat in his chamber; and with him were Owain the son of Urien, and Kynon the son of Clydno, and Kai the son of Kyner; and Gwenhwyvar and her handmaidens at needlework by the window. And if it should be said that there was a porter at Arthur's palace, there was none. Glewlwyd Gavaelvawr was there, acting as porter, to welcome guests and strangers, and to receive them with honour, and to inform them of the manners and customs of the Court; and to direct those who came to the Hall or to the presence-chamber, and those who came to take up their lodging.

In the centre of the chamber King Arthur sat upon a seat of green rushes, over which was spread a covering of flame-coloured satin, and a cushion of red satin was under his elbow.

Then Arthur spoke, "If I thought you would not disparage me," said he, "I would sleep while I wait for my repast; and you can entertain one another with relating tales, and can obtain a flagon of mead and some meat from Kai." And the King went to sleep. And Kynon the son of Clydno asked Kai for that which Arthur had promised them. "I, too, will have the good tale which he promised to me," said Kai. "Nay," answered Kynon, "fairer will it be for thee to fulfill Arthur's behest, in the first place, and then we will tell thee the best tale that we know." So Kai went to the kitchen and to the mead- cellar, and returned bearing a flagon of mead and a golden goblet, and a handful of skewers, upon which were broiled collops of meat. Then they ate the collops and began to drink the mead. "Now," said Kai, "it is time for you to give me my story." "Kynon," said Owain, "do thou pay to Kai the tale that is his due." "Truly," said Kynon, "thou are older, and art a better teller of tales, and hast seen more marvellous things than I; do thou therefore pay Kai his tale." "Begin thyself," quoth Owain, "with the best that thou knowest." "I will do so," answered Kynon.

"I was the only son of my mother and father, and I was exceedingly aspiring, and my daring was very great. I thought there was no enterprise in the world too mighty for me, and after I had achieved all the adventures that were in my own country, I equipped myself, and set forth to journey through deserts and distant regions. And at length it chanced that I came to the fairest valley in the world, wherein were trees of equal growth; and a river ran through the valley, and a path was by the side of the river. And I followed the path until mid-day, and continued my journey along the remainder of the valley until the evening; and at the extremity of a plain I came to a large and lustrous Castle, at the foot of which was a torrent. And I approached the Castle, and there I beheld two youths with yellow curling hair, each with a frontlet of gold upon his head, and clad in a garment of yellow satin, and they had gold clasps upon their insteps. In the hand of each of them was an ivory bow, strung with the sinews of the stag; and their arrows had shafts of the bone of the whale, and were winged with peacock's feathers; the shafts also had golden heads. And they had daggers with blades of gold, and with hilts of the bone of the whale. And they were shooting their daggers.

"And a little way from them I saw a man in the prime of life, with his beard newly shorn, clad in a robe and a mantle of yellow satin; and round the top of his mantle was a band of gold lace. On his feet were shoes of variegated leather, fastened by two bosses of gold. When I saw him, I went towards him and saluted him, and such was his courtesy that he no sooner received my greeting than he returned it. And he went with me towards the Castle. Now there were no dwellers in the Castle except those who were in one hall. And there I saw four-and-twenty damsels, embroidering satin at a window. And this I tell thee, Kai, that the least fair of them was fairer than the fairest maid thou hast ever beheld in the Island of Britain, and the least lovely of them was more lovely than Gwenhwyvar, the wife of Arthur, when she has appeared loveliest at the Offering, on the day of the Nativity, or at the feast of Easter. They rose up at my coming, and six of them took my horse, and divested me of my armour; and six others took my arms, and washed them in a vessel until they were perfectly bright. And the third six spread cloths upon the tables and prepared meat. And the fourth six took off my soiled garments, and placed others upon me; namely, an under-vest and a doublet of fine linen, and a robe, and a surcoat, and a mantle of yellow satin with a broad gold band upon the mantle. And they placed cushions both beneath and around me, with coverings of red linen; and I sat down. Now the six maidens who had taken my horse, unharnessed him, as well as if they had been the best squires in the Island of Britain. Then, behold, they brought bowls of silver wherein was water to wash, and towels of linen, some green and some white; and I washed. And in a little while the man sat down to the table. And I sat next to him, and below me sat all the maidens, except those who waited on us. And the table was of silver, and the cloths upon the table were of linen; and no vessel was served upon the table that was not either of gold or of silver, or of buffalo-horn. And our meat was brought to us. And verily, Kai, I saw there every sort of meat and every sort of liquor that I have ever seen elsewhere; but the meat and the liquor were better served there than I have ever seen them in any other place.

"Until the repast was half over, neither the man nor any one of the damsels spoke a single word to me; but when the man perceived that it would be more agreeable to me to converse than to eat any more, he began to inquire of me who I was. I said I was glad to find that there was some one who would discourse with me, and that it was not considered so great a crime at that Court for people to hold converse together. 'Chieftain,' said the man, 'we would have talked to thee sooner, but we feared to disturb thee during thy repast; now, however, we will discourse.' Then I told the man who I was, and what was the cause of my journey; and said that I was seeking whether any one was superior to me, or whether I could gain the mastery over all. The man looked upon me, and he smiled and said, 'If I did not fear to distress thee too much, I would show thee that which thou seekest.' Upon this I became anxious and sorrowful, and when the man perceived it, he said, 'If thou wouldest rather that I should show thee thy disadvantage than thine advantage, I will do so. Sleep here to-night, and in the morning arise early, and take the road upwards through the valley until thou reachest the wood through which thou camest hither. A little way within the wood thou wilt meet with a road branching off to the right, by which thou must proceed, until thou comest to a large sheltered glade with a mound in the centre. And thou wilt see a black man of great stature on the top of the mound. He is not smaller in size than two of the men of this world. He has but one foot; and one eye in the middle of his forehead. And he has a club of iron, and it is certain that there are no two men in the world who would not find their burden in that club. And he is not a comely man, but on the contrary he is exceedingly ill-favoured; and he is the woodward of that wood. And thou wilt see a thousand wild animals grazing around him. Inquire of him the way out of the glade, and he will reply to thee briefly, and will point out the road by which thou shalt find that which thou art in quest of.'

"And long seemed that night to me. And the next morning I arose and equipped myself, and mounted my horse, and proceeded straight through the valley to the wood; and I followed the cross-road which the man had pointed out to me, till at length I arrived at the glade. And there was I three times more astonished at the number of wild animals that I beheld, than the man had said I should be. And the black man was there, sitting upon the top of the mound. Huge of stature as the man had told me that he was, I found him to exceed by far the description he had given me of him. As for the iron club which the man had told me was a burden for two men, I am certain, Kai, that it would be a heavy weight for four warriors to lift; and this was in the black man's hand. And he only spoke to me in answer to my questions. Then I asked him what power he held over those animals. 'I will show thee, little man,' said he. And he took his club in his hand, and with it he struck a stag a great blow so that he brayed vehemently, and at his braying the animals came together, as numerous as the stars in the sky, so that it was difficult for me to find room in the glade to stand among them. There were serpents, and dragons, and divers sorts of animals. And he looked at them, and bade them go and feed; and they bowed their heads, and did him homage as vassals to their lord.

"Then the black man said to me, 'Seest thou now, little man, what power I hold over these animals?' Then I inquired of him the way, and he became very rough in his manner to me; however, he asked me whither I would go? And when I told him who I was and what I sought, he directed me. 'Take,' said he, 'that path that leads towards the head of the glade, and ascend the wooded steep until thou comest to its summit; and there thou wilt find an open space like to a large valley, and in the midst of it a tall tree, whose branches are greener than the greenest pine-trees. Under this tree is a fountain, and by the side of the fountain a marble slab, and on the marble slab a silver bowl, attached by a chain of silver, so that it may not be carried away. Take the bowl and throw a bowlful of water upon the slab, and thou wilt hear a mighty peal of thunder, so that thou wilt think that heaven and earth are trembling with its fury. With the thunder there will come a shower so severe that it will be scarce possible for thee to endure it and live. And the shower will be of hailstones; and after the shower, the weather will become fair, but every leaf that was upon the tree will have been carried away by the shower. Then a flight of birds will come and alight upon the tree; and in thine own country thou didst never hear a strain so sweet as that which they will sing. And at the moment thou art most delighted with the song of the birds, thou wilt hear a murmuring and complaining coming towards thee along the valley. And thou wilt see a knight upon a coal-black horse, clothed in black velvet, and with a pennon of black linen upon his lance; and he will ride unto thee to encounter thee with the utmost speed. If thou fleest from him he will overtake thee, and if thou abidest there, as sure as thou art a mounted knight, he will leave thee on foot. And if thou dost not find trouble in that adventure, thou needest not seek it during the rest of thy life.'

"So I journeyed on, until I reached the summit of the steep, and there I found everything as the black man had described it to me. And I went up to the tree, and beneath it I saw the fountain, and by its side the marble slab, and the silver bowl fastened by the chain. Then I took the bowl, and cast a bowlful of water upon the slab; and thereupon, behold, the thunder came, much more violent than the black man had led me to expect; and after the thunder came the shower; and of a truth I tell thee, Kai, that there is neither man nor beast that can endure that shower and live. For not one of those hailstones would be stopped, either by the flesh or by the skin, until it had reached the bone. I turned my horse's flank towards the shower, and placed the beak of my shield over his head and neck, while I held the upper part of it over my own head. And thus I withstood the shower. When I looked on the tree there was not a single leaf upon it, and then the sky became clear, and with that, behold the birds lighted upon the tree, and sang. And truly, Kai, I never heard any melody equal to that, either before or since. And when I was most charmed with listening to the birds, lo, a murmuring voice was heard through the valley, approaching me and saying, 'Oh, Knight, what has brought thee hither? What evil have I done to thee, that thou shouldst act towards me and my possessions as thou hast this day? Dost thou not know that the shower to-day has left in my dominions neither man nor beast alive that was exposed to it?' And thereupon, behold, a Knight on a black horse appeared, clothed in jet-black velvet, and with a tabard of black linen about him. And we charged each other, and, as the onset was furious, it was not long before I was overthrown. Then the Knight passed the shaft of his lance through the bridle rein of my horse, and rode off with the two horses, leaving me where I was. And he did not even bestow so much notice upon me as to imprison me, nor did he despoil me of my arms. So I returned along the road by which I had come. And when I reached the glade where the black man was, I confess to thee, Kai, it is a marvel that I did not melt down into a liquid pool, through the shame that I felt at the black man's derision. And that night I came to the same castle where I had spent the night preceding. And I was more agreeably entertained that night than I had been the night before; and I was better feasted, and I conversed freely with the inmates of the castle, and none of them alluded to my expedition to the fountain, neither did I mention it to any; and I remained there that night. When I arose on the morrow, I found, ready saddled, a dark bay palfrey, with nostrils as red as scarlet; and after putting on my armour, and leaving there my blessing, I returned to my own Court. And that horse I still possess, and he is in the stable yonder. And I declare that I would not part with him for the best palfrey in the Island of Britain.

"Now of a truth, Kai, no man ever before confessed to an adventure so much to his own discredit, and verily it seems strange to me, that neither before nor since have I heard of any person besides myself who knew of this adventure, and that the subject of it should exist within King Arthur's dominions, without any other person lighting upon it."

"Now," quoth Owain, "would it not be well to go and endeavour to discover that place?"

"By the hand of my friend," said Kai, "often dost thou utter that with thy tongue which thou wouldst not make good with thy deeds."

"In very truth," said Gwenhwyvar, "it were better thou wert hanged, Kai, than to use such uncourteous speech towards a man like Owain."

"By the hand of my friend, good Lady," said Kai, "thy praise of Owain is not greater than mine."

With that Arthur awoke, and asked if he had not been sleeping a little.

"Yes, Lord," answered Owain, "thou hast slept awhile."

"Is it time for us to go to meat?"

"It is, Lord," said Owain.

Then the horn for washing was sounded, and the King and all his household sat down to eat. And when the meal was ended, Owain withdrew to his lodging, and made ready his horse and his arms.

On the morrow, with the dawn of day, he put on his armour, and mounted his charger, and travelled through distant lands and over desert mountains. And at length he arrived at the valley which Kynon had described to him; and he was certain that it was the same that he sought. And journeying along the valley by the side of the river, he followed its course till he came to the plain and within sight of the Castle. When he approached the Castle, he saw the youths shooting their daggers in the place where Kynon had seen them, and the yellow man, to whom the Castle belonged, standing hard by. And no sooner had Owain saluted the yellow man than he was saluted by him in return.

And he went forward towards the Castle, and there he saw the chamber, and when he had entered the chamber he beheld the maidens working at satin embroidery, in chairs of gold. And their beauty and their comeliness seemed to Owain far greater than Kynon had represented to him. And they rose to wait upon Owain, as they had done to Kynon, and the meal which they set before him gave more satisfaction to Owain than it had done to Kynon.

About the middle of the repast, the yellow man asked Owain the object of his journey. And Owain made it known to him, and said, "I am in quest of the Knight who guards the fountain." Upon this the yellow man smiled, and said that he was as loth to point out that adventure to Owain as he had been to Kynon. However, he described the whole to Owain, and they retired to rest.

The next morning Owain found his horse made ready for him by the damsels, and he set forward and came to the glade where the black man was. And the stature of the black man seemed more wonderful to Owain than it had done to Kynon, and Owain asked of him his road, and he showed it to him. And Owain followed the road, as Kynon had done, till he came to the green tree; and he beheld the fountain, and the slab beside the fountain, with the bowl upon it. And Owain took the bowl, and threw a bowlful of water upon the slab. And, lo, the thunder was heard, and after the thunder came the shower, much more violent than Kynon had described, and after the shower the sky became bright. And when Owain looked at the tree, there was not one leaf upon it. And immediately the birds came, and settled upon the tree, and sang. And when their song was most pleasing to Owain, he beheld a Knight coming towards him through the valley, and he prepared to receive him; and encountered him violently. Having broken both their lances, they drew their swords, and fought blade to blade. Then Owain struck the Knight a blow through his helmet, head-piece and visor, and through the skin, and the flesh, and the bone, until it wounded the very brain. Then the black Knight felt that he had received a mortal wound, upon which he turned his horse's head, and fled. And Owain pursued him, and followed close upon him, although he was not near enough to strike him with his sword. Thereupon Owain descried a vast and resplendent Castle. And they came to the Castle gate. And the black Knight was allowed to enter, and the portcullis was let fall upon Owain; and it struck his horse behind the saddle, and cut him in two, and carried away the rowels of the spurs that were upon Owain's heels. And the portcullis descended to the floor. And the rowels of the spurs and part of the horse were without, and Owain with the other part of the horse remained between the two gates, and the inner gate was closed, so that Owain could not go thence; and Owain was in a perplexing situation. And while he was in this state, he could see through an aperture in the gate, a street facing him, with a row of houses on each side. And he beheld a maiden, with yellow curling hair, and a frontlet of gold upon her head; and she was clad in a dress of yellow satin, and on her feet were shoes of variegated leather. And she approached the gate, and desired that it should be opened. "Heaven knows, Lady," said Owain, "it is no more possible for me to open to thee from hence, than it is for thee to set me free." "Truly," said the damsel, "it is very sad that thou canst not be released, and every woman ought to succour thee, for I never saw one more faithful in the service of ladies than thou. As a friend thou art the most sincere, and as a lover the most devoted. Therefore," quoth she, "whatever is in my power to do for thy release, I will do it. Take this ring and put it on thy finger, with the stone inside thy hand; and close thy hand upon the stone. And as long as thou concealest it, it will conceal thee. When they have consulted together, they will come forth to fetch thee, in order to put thee to death; and they will be much grieved that they cannot find thee. And I will await thee on the horseblock yonder; and thou wilt be able to see me, though I cannot see thee; therefore come and place thy hand upon my shoulder, that I may know that thou art near me. And by the way that I go hence, do thou accompany me."

Then she went away from Owain, and he did all that the maiden had told him. And the people of the Castle came to seek Owain, to put him to death, and when they found nothing but the half of his horse, they were sorely grieved.

And Owain vanished from among them, and went to the maiden, and placed his hand upon her shoulder; whereupon she set off, and Owain followed her, until they came to the door of a large and beautiful chamber, and the maiden opened it, and they went in, and closed the door. And Owain looked around the chamber, and behold there was not even a single nail in it that was not painted with gorgeous colours; and there was not a single panel that had not sundry images in gold portrayed upon it.

The maiden kindled a fire, and took water in a silver bowl, and put a towel of white linen on her shoulder, and gave Owain water to wash. Then she placed before him a silver table, inlaid with gold; upon which was a cloth of yellow linen; and she brought him food. And of a truth, Owain had never seen any kind of meat that was not there in abundance, but it was better cooked there than he had ever found it in any other place. Nor did he ever see so excellent a display of meat and drink, as there. And there was not one vessel from which he was served, that was not of gold or of silver. And Owain ate and drank, until late in the afternoon, when lo, they heard a mighty clamour in the Castle; and Owain asked the maiden what that outcry was. "They are administering extreme unction," said she, "to the Nobleman who owns the Castle." And Owain went to sleep.

The couch which the maiden had prepared for him was meet for Arthur himself; it was of scarlet, and fur, and satin, and sendal, and fine linen. In the middle of the night they heard a woful outcry. "What outcry again is this?" said Owain. "The Nobleman who owned the Castle is now dead," said the maiden. And a little after daybreak, they heard an exceeding loud clamour and wailing. And Owain asked the maiden what was the cause of it. "They are bearing to the church the body of the Nobleman who owned the Castle."

And Owain rose up, and clothed himself, and opened a window of the chamber, and looked towards the Castle; and he could see neither the bounds, nor the extent of the hosts that filled the streets. And they were fully armed; and a vast number of women were with them, both on horseback and on foot; and all the ecclesiastics in the city, singing. And it seemed to Owain that the sky resounded with the vehemence of their cries, and with the noise of the trumpets, and with the singing of the ecclesiastics. In the midst of the throng, he beheld the bier, over which was a veil of white linen; and wax tapers were burning beside and around it, and none that supported the bier was lower in rank than a powerful Baron.

Never did Owain see an assemblage so gorgeous with satin, and silk, and sendal. And following the train, he beheld a lady with yellow hair falling over her shoulders, and stained with blood; and about her a dress of yellow satin, which was torn. Upon her feet were shoes of variegated leather. And it was a marvel that the ends of her fingers were not bruised, from the violence with which she smote her hands together. Truly she would have been the fairest lady Owain ever saw, had she been in her usual guise. And her cry was louder than the shout of the men, or the clamour of the trumpets. No sooner had he beheld the lady, than he became inflamed with her love, so that it took entire possession of him.

Then he inquired of the maiden who the lady was. "Heaven knows," replied the maiden, "she may be said to be the fairest, and the most chaste, and the most liberal, and the wisest, and the most noble of women. And she is my mistress; and she is called the Countess of the Fountain, the wife of him whom thou didst slay yesterday." "Verily," said Owain, "she is the woman that I love best." "Verily," said the maiden, "she shall also love thee not a little."

And with that the maid arose, and kindled a fire, and filled a pot with water, and placed it to warm; and she brought a towel of white linen, and placed it around Owain's neck; and she took a goblet of ivory, and a silver basin, and filled them with warm water, wherewith she washed Owain's head. Then she opened a wooden casket, and drew forth a razor, whose haft was of ivory, and upon which were two rivets of gold. And she shaved his beard, and she dried his head, and his throat, with the towel. Then she rose up from before Owain, and brought him to eat. And truly Owain had never so good a meal, nor was he ever so well served.

When he had finished his repast, the maiden arranged his couch. "Come here," said she, "and sleep, and I will go and woo for thee." And Owain went to sleep, and the maiden shut the door of the chamber after her, and went towards the Castle. When she came there, she found nothing but mourning, and sorrow; and the Countess in her chamber could not bear the sight of any one through grief. Luned came and saluted her, but the Countess answered her not. And the maiden bent down towards her, and said, "What aileth thee, that thou answerest no one to-day?" "Luned," said the Countess, "what change hath befallen thee, that thou hast not come to visit me in my grief? It was wrong in thee, and I having made thee rich; it was wrong in thee that thou didst not come to see me in my distress. That was wrong in thee." "Truly," said Luned, "I thought thy good sense was greater than I find it to be. Is it well for thee to mourn after that good man, or for anything else, that thou canst not have?" "I declare to heaven," said the Countess, "that in the whole world there is not a man equal to him." "Not so," said Luned, "for an ugly man would be as good as, or better than he." "I declare to heaven," said the Countess, "that were it not repugnant to me to cause to be put to death one whom I have brought up, I would have thee executed, for making such a comparison to me. As it is, I will banish thee." "I am glad," said Luned, "that thou hast no other cause to do so, than that I would have been of service to thee where thou didst not know what was to thine advantage. And henceforth evil betide whichever of us shall make the first advance towards reconciliation to the other; whether I should seek an invitation from thee, or thou of thine own accord shouldst send to invite me."

With that Luned went forth: and the Countess arose and followed her to the door of the chamber, and began coughing loudly. And when Luned looked back, the Countess beckoned to her; and she returned to the Countess. "In truth," said the

Countess, "evil is thy disposition; but if thou knowest what is to my advantage, declare it to me." "I will do so," quoth she.

"Thou knowest that except by warfare and arms it is impossible for thee to preserve thy possessions; delay not, therefore, to seek some one who can defend them." "And how can I do that?" said the Countess. "I will tell thee," said Luned. "Unless thou canst defend the fountain, thou canst not maintain thy dominions; and no one can defend the fountain, except it be a knight of Arthur's household; and I will go to Arthur's Court, and ill betide me, if I return thence without a warrior who can guard the fountain as well as, or even better than, he who defended it formerly." "That will be hard to perform," said the Countess. "Go, however, and make proof of that which thou hast promised."

Luned set out, under the pretence of going to Arthur's Court; but she went back to the chamber where she had left Owain; and she tarried there with him as long as it might have taken her to have travelled to the Court of King Arthur. And at the end of that time, she apparelled herself and went to visit the Countess. And the Countess was much rejoiced when she saw her, and inquired what news she brought from the Court. "I bring thee the best of news," said Luned, "for I have compassed the object of my mission. When wilt thou, that I should present to thee the chieftain who has come with me hither?" "Bring him here to visit me to-morrow, at mid-day," said the Countess, "and I will cause the town to be assembled by that time."

And Luned returned home. And the next day, at noon, Owain arrayed himself in a coat, and a surcoat, and a mantle of yellow satin, upon which was a broad band of gold lace; and on his feet were high shoes of variegated leather, which were fastened by golden clasps, in the form of lions. And they proceeded to the chamber of the Countess.

Right glad was the Countess of their coming, and she gazed steadfastly upon Owain, and said, "Luned, this knight has not the look of a traveller." "What harm is there in that, lady?" said Luned. "I am certain," said the Countess, "that no other man than this chased the soul from the body of my lord." "So much the better for thee, lady," said Luned, "for had he not been stronger than thy lord he could not have deprived him of life. There is no remedy for that which is past, be it as it may." "Go back to thine abode," said the Countess, "and I will take counsel."

The next day the Countess caused all her subjects to assemble, and showed them that her earldom was left defenceless, and that it could not be protected but with horse and arms, and military skill. "Therefore," said she, "this is what I offer for your choice: either let one of you take me, or give your consent for me to take a husband from elsewhere to defend my dominions."

So they came to the determination that it was better that she should have permission to marry some one from elsewhere; and, thereupon, she sent for the bishops and archbishops to celebrate her nuptials with Owain. And the men of the earldom did Owain homage.

And Owain defended the Fountain with lance and sword. And this is the manner in which he defended it: Whensoever a knight came there he overthrew him, and sold him for his full worth, and what he thus gained he divided among his barons and his knights; and no man in the whole world could be more beloved than he was by his subjects. And it was thus for the space of three years.

It befell that as Gwalchmai went forth one day with King Arthur, he perceived him to be very sad and sorrowful. And Gwalchmai was much grieved to see Arthur in this state; and he questioned him, saying, "Oh, my lord! what has befallen thee?" "In sooth, Gwalchmai," said Arthur, "I am grieved concerning Owain, whom I have lost these three years, and I shall certainly die if the fourth year passes without my seeing him. Now I am sure, that it is through the tale which Kynon the son of Clydno related, that I have lost Owain." "There is no need for thee," said Gwalchmai, "to summon to arms thy whole dominions on this account, for thou thyself and the men of thy household will be able to avenge Owain, if he be slain; or to set him free, if he be in prison; and, if alive, to bring him back with thee." And it was settled according to what Gwalchmai had said.

Then Arthur and the men of his household prepared to go and seek Owain, and their number was three thousand, besides their attendants. And Kynon the son of Clydno acted as their guide. And Arthur came to the Castle where Kynon had been before, and when he came there the youths were shooting in the same place, and the yellow man was standing hard by. When the yellow man saw Arthur he greeted him, and invited him to the Castle; and Arthur accepted his invitation, and they entered the Castle together. And great as was the number of his retinue, their presence was scarcely observed in the Castle, so vast was its extent. And the maidens rose up to wait on them, and the service of the maidens appeared to them all to excel any attendance they had ever met with; and even the pages who had charge of the horses were no worse served, that night, than Arthur himself would have been in his own palace.

The next morning Arthur set out thence, with Kynon for his guide, and came to the place where the black man was. And the stature of the black man was more surprising to Arthur than it had been represented to him. And they came to the top of the wooded steep, and traversed the valley till they reached the green tree, where they saw the fountain, and the bowl, and the slab. And upon that, Kai came to Arthur and spoke to him. "My lord," said he, "I know the meaning of all this, and my request is, that thou wilt permit me to throw the water on the slab, and to receive the first adventure that may befall." And Arthur gave him leave.

Then Kai threw a bowlful of water upon the slab, and immediately there came the thunder, and after the thunder the shower. And such a thunderstorm they had never known before, and many of the attendants who were in Arthur's train were killed by the shower. After the shower had ceased the sky became clear; and on looking at the tree they beheld it completely leafless. Then the birds descended upon the tree, and the song of the birds was far sweeter than any strain they had ever heard before. Then they beheld a knight on a coal-black horse, clothed in black satin, coming rapidly towards them. And Kai met him and encountered him, and it was not long before Kai was overthrown. And the knight withdrew, and Arthur and his host encamped for the night.

And when they arose in the morning, they perceived the signal of combat upon the lance of the Knight. And Kai came to Arthur, and spoke to him: "My lord," said he, "though I was overthrown yesterday, if it seem good to thee, I would gladly meet the Knight again to-day." "Thou mayst do so," said Arthur. And Kai went towards the Knight. And on the spot he overthrew Kai, and struck him with the head of his lance in the forehead, so that it broke his helmet and the head-piece, and pierced the skin and the flesh, the breadth of the spear-head, even to the bone. And Kai returned to his companions.

After this, all the household of Arthur went forth, one after the other, to combat the Knight, until there was not one that was not overthrown by him, except Arthur and Gwalchmai. And Arthur armed himself to encounter the Knight. "Oh, my lord," said Gwalchmai, "permit me to fight with him first." And Arthur permitted him. And he went forth to meet the Knight, having over himself and his horse a satin robe of honour which had been sent him by the daughter of the Earl of Rhangyw, and in this dress he was not known by any of the host. And they charged each other, and fought all that day until the evening, and neither of them was able to unhorse the other.

The next day they fought with strong lances, and neither of them could obtain the mastery.

And the third day they fought with exceeding strong lances. And they were incensed with rage, and fought furiously, even until noon. And they gave each other such a shock that the girths of their horses were broken, so that they fell over their horses' cruppers to the ground. And they rose up speedily, and drew their swords, and resumed the combat; and the multitude that witnessed their encounter felt assured that they had never before seen two men so valiant or so powerful. And had it been midnight, it would have been light from the fire that flashed from their weapons. And the Knight gave Gwalchmai a blow that turned his helmet from off his face, so that the Knight knew that it was Gwalchmai. Then Owain said, "My lord Gwalchmai, I did not know thee for my cousin, owing to the robe of honour that enveloped thee; take my sword and my arms." Said Gwalchmai, "Thou, Owain, art the victor; take thou my sword." And with that Arthur saw that they were conversing, and advanced towards them. "My lord Arthur," said Gwalchmai, "here is Owain, who has vanquished me, and will not take my arms." "My lord," said Owain, "it is he that has vanquished me, and he will not take my sword." "Give me your swords," said Arthur, "and then neither of you has vanquished the other." Then Owain put his arms around Arthur's neck, and they embraced. And all the host hurried forward to see Owain, and to embrace him; and there was nigh being a loss of life, so great was the press.

And they retired that night, and the next day Arthur prepared to depart. "My lord," said Owain, "this is not well of thee; for I have been absent from thee these three years, and during all that time, up to this very day, I have been preparing a banquet for thee, knowing that thou wouldst come to seek me. Tarry with me, therefore, until thou and thy attendants have recovered the fatigues of the journey, and have been anointed."

And they all proceeded to the Castle of the Countess of the Fountain, and the banquet which had been three years preparing was consumed in three months. Never had they a more delicious or agreeable banquet. And Arthur prepared to depart. Then he sent an embassy to the Countess, to beseech her to permit Owain to go with him for the space of three months, that he might show him to the nobles and the fair dames of the Island of Britain. And the Countess gave her consent, although it was very painful to her. So Owain came with Arthur to the Island of Britain. And when he was once more amongst his kindred and friends, he remained three years, instead of three months, with them.

And as Owain one day sat at meat, in the city of Caerlleon upon Usk, behold a damsel entered upon a bay horse, with a curling mane and covered with foam, and the bridle and so much as was seen of the saddle were of gold. And the damsel was arrayed in a dress of yellow satin. And she came up to Owain, and took the ring from off his hand. "Thus," said she, "shall be treated the deceiver, the traitor, the faithless, the disgraced, and the beardless." And she turned her horse's head and departed.

Then his adventure came to Owain's remembrance, and he was sorrowful; and having finished eating he went to his own abode and made preparations that night. And the next day he arose but did not go to the Court, but wandered to the distant parts of the earth and to uncultivated mountains. And he remained there until all his apparel was worn out, and his body was wasted away, and his hair was grown long. And he went about with the wild beasts and fed with them, until they became familiar with him; but at length he grew so weak that he could no longer bear them company. Then he descended from the mountains to the valley, and came to a park that was the fairest in the world, and belonged to a widowed Countess.

One day the Countess and her maidens went forth to walk by a lake, that was in the middle of the park. And they saw the form of a man. And they were terrified. Nevertheless they went near him, and touched him, and looked at him. And they saw that there was life in him, though he was exhausted by the heat of the sun. And the Countess returned to the Castle, and took a flask full of precious ointment, and gave it to one of her maidens. "Go with this," said she, "and take with thee yonder horse and clothing, and place them near the man we saw just now. And anoint him with this balsam, near his heart; and if there is life in him, he will arise through the efficacy of this balsam. Then watch what he will do."

And the maiden departed from her, and poured the whole of the balsam upon Owain, and left the horse and the garments hard by, and went a little way off, and hid herself to watch him. In a short time she saw him begin to move his arms; and he rose up, and looked at his person, and became ashamed of the unseemliness of his appearance. Then he perceived the horse and the garments that were near him. And he crept forward till he was able to draw the garments to him from off the saddle. And he clothed himself, and with difficulty mounted the horse. Then the damsel discovered herself to him, and saluted him. And he was rejoiced when he saw her, and inquired of her, what land and what territory that was. "Truly," said the maiden, "a widowed Countess owns yonder Castle; at the death of her husband, he left her two Earldoms, but at this day she has but this one dwelling that has not been wrested from her by a young Earl, who is her neighbour, because she refused to become his wife." "That is pity," said Owain. And he and the maiden proceeded to the Castle; and he alighted there, and the maiden conducted him to a pleasant chamber, and kindled a fire and left him.

And the maiden came to the Countess, and gave the flask into her hand. "Ha! maiden," said the Countess, "where is all the balsam?" "Have I not used it all?" said she. "Oh, maiden," said the Countess, "I cannot easily forgive thee this; it is sad for me to have wasted seven-score pounds' worth of precious ointment upon a stranger whom I know not. However, maiden, wait thou upon him, until he is quite recovered."

And the maiden did so, and furnished him with meat and drink, and fire, and lodging, and medicaments, until he was well again. And in three months he was restored to his former guise, and became even more comely than he had ever been before.

One day Owain heard a great tumult, and a sound of arms in the Castle, and he inquired of the maiden the cause thereof. "The Earl," said she, "whom I mentioned to thee, has come before the Castle, with a numerous army, to subdue the Countess." And Owain inquired of her whether the Countess had a horse and arms in her possession. "She has the best in the world," said the maiden. "Wilt thou go and request the loan of a horse and arms for me," said Owain, "that I may go and look at this army?" "I will," said the maiden.

And she came to the Countess, and told her what Owain had said. And the Countess laughed. "Truly," said she, "I will even give him a horse and arms for ever; such a horse and such arms had he never yet, and I am glad that they should be taken by him to-day, lest my enemies should have them against my will to-morrow. Yet I know not what he would do with them."

The Countess bade them bring out a beautiful black steed, upon which was a beechen saddle, and a suit of armour, for man and horse. And Owain armed himself, and mounted the horse, and went forth, attended by two pages completely equipped, with horses and arms. And when they came near to the Earl's army, they could see neither its extent nor its extremity. And Owain asked the pages in which troop the Earl was. "In yonder troop," said they, "in which are four yellow standards. Two of them are before, and two behind him." "Now," said Owain, "do you return and await me near the portal of the Castle." So they returned, and Owain pressed forward until he met the Earl. And Owain drew him completely out of his saddle, and turned his horse's head towards the Castle, and though it was with difficulty, he brought the Earl to the portal, where the pages awaited him. And in they came. And Owain presented the Earl as a gift to the Countess. And said to her, "Behold a requital to thee for thy blessed balsam."

The army encamped around the Castle. And the Earl restored to the Countess the two Earldoms he had taken from her, as a ransom for his life; and for his freedom he gave her the half of his own dominions, and all his gold, and his silver, and his jewels, besides hostages.

And Owain took his departure. And the Countess and all her subjects besought him to remain, but Owain chose rather to wander through distant lands and deserts.

And as he journeyed, he heard a loud yelling in a wood. And it was repeated a second and a third time. And Owain went towards the spot, and beheld a huge craggy mound, in the middle of the wood; on the side of which was a grey rock. And there was a cleft in the rock, and a serpent was within the cleft. And near the rock stood a black lion, and every time the lion sought to go thence, the serpent darted towards him to attack him. And Owain unsheathed his sword, and drew near to the rock; and as the serpent sprang out, he struck him with his sword, and cut him in two. And he dried his sword, and went on his way, as before. But behold the lion followed him, and played about him, as though it had been a greyhound that he had reared.

They proceeded thus throughout the day, until the evening. And when it was time for Owain to take his rest, he dismounted, and turned his horse loose in a flat and wooded meadow. And he struck fire, and when the fire was kindled, the lion brought him fuel enough to last for three nights. And the lion disappeared. And presently the lion returned, bearing a fine large roebuck. And he threw it down before Owain, who went towards the fire with it.

And Owain took the roebuck, and skinned it, and placed collops of its flesh upon skewers, around the fire. The rest of the buck he gave to the lion to devour. While he was doing this, he heard a deep sigh near him, and a second, and a third. And Owain called out to know whether the sigh he heard proceeded from a mortal; and he received answer that it did. "Who art thou?" said Owain. "Truly," said the voice, "I am Luned, the handmaiden of the Countess of the Fountain." "And what dost thou here?"

said Owain. "I am imprisoned," said she, "on account of the knight who came from Arthur's Court, and married the Countess. And he stayed a short time with her, but he afterwards departed for the Court of Arthur, and has not returned since. And he was the friend I loved best in the world. And two of the pages in the Countess's chamber traduced him, and called him a deceiver. And I told them that they two were not a match for him alone. So they imprisoned me in the stone vault, and said that I should be put to death, unless he came himself to deliver me, by a certain day; and that is no further off than the day after to-morrow. And I have no one to send to seek him for me. And his name is Owain the son of Urien." "And art thou certain that if that knight knew all this, he would come to thy rescue?" "I am most certain of it," said she.

When the collops were cooked, Owain divided them into two parts, between himself and the maiden; and after they had eaten, they talked together, until the day dawned. And the next morning Owain inquired of the damsel, if there was any place where he could get food and entertainment for that night. "There is, Lord," said she; "cross over yonder, and go along the side of the river, and in a short time thou wilt see a great Castle, in which are many towers, and the Earl who owns that Castle is the most hospitable man in the world. There thou mayst spend the night."

Never did sentinel keep stricter watch over his lord, than the lion that night over Owain.

And Owain accoutred his horse, and passed across by the ford, and came in sight of the Castle. And he entered it, and was honourably received. And his horse was well cared for, and plenty of fodder was placed before him. Then the lion went and lay down in the horse's manger; so that none of the people of the Castle dared to approach him. The treatment which Owain met with there was such as he had never known elsewhere, for every one was as sorrowful as though death had been upon him. And they went to meat; and the Earl sat upon one side of Owain, and on the other side his only daughter. And Owain had never seen any more lovely than she. Then the lion came and placed himself between Owain's feet, and he fed him with every kind of food that he took himself. And he never saw anything equal to the sadness of the people.

In the middle of the repast the Earl began to bid Owain welcome. "Then," said Owain, "behold, it is time for thee to be cheerful." "Heaven knows," said the Earl, "that it is not thy coming that makes us sorrowful, but we have cause enough for sadness and care." "What is that?" said Owain. "I have two sons," replied the Earl, "and yesterday they went to the mountains to hunt. Now there is on the mountain a monster who kills men and devours them, and he seized my sons; and to-morrow is the time he has fixed to be here, and he threatens that he will then slay my sons before my eyes, unless I will deliver into his hands this my daughter. He has the form of a man, but in stature he is no less than a giant."

"Truly," said Owain, "that is lamentable. And which wilt thou do?" "Heaven knows," said the Earl, "it will be better that my sons should be slain against my will, than that I should voluntarily give up my daughter to him to ill-treat and destroy." Then they talked about other things, and Owain stayed there that night.

The next morning they heard an exceeding great clamour, which was caused by the coming of the giant with the two youths. And the Earl was anxious both to protect his Castle and to release his two sons. Then Owain put on his armour and went forth to encounter the giant, and the lion followed him. And when the giant saw that Owain was armed, he rushed towards him and attacked him. And the lion fought with the giant much more fiercely than Owain did. "Truly," said the giant, "I should find no difficulty in fighting with thee, were it not for the animal that is with thee." Upon that Owain took the lion back to the Castle and shut the gate upon him, and then he returned to fight the giant, as before. And the lion roared very loud, for he heard that it went hard with Owain. And he climbed up till he reached the top of the Earl's hall, and thence he got to the top of the Castle, and he sprang down from the walls and went and joined Owain. And the lion gave the giant a stroke with his paw, which tore him from his shoulder to his hip, and his heart was laid bare, and the giant fell down dead. Then Owain restored the two youths to their father.

The Earl besought Owain to remain with him, and he would not, but set forward towards the meadow where Luned was. And when he came there he saw a great fire kindled, and two youths with beautiful curling auburn hair were leading the maiden to cast her into the fire. And Owain asked them what charge they had against her. And they told him of the compact that was between them, as the maiden had done the night before. "And," said they, "Owain has failed her, therefore we are taking her to be burnt." "Truly," said Owain, "he is a good knight, and if he knew that the maiden was in such peril, I marvel that he came not to her rescue; but if you will accept me in his stead, I will do battle with you." "We will," said the youths, "by him who made us."

And they attacked Owain, and he was hard beset by them. And with that the lion came to Owain's assistance, and they two got the better of the young men. And they said to him, "Chieftain, it was not agreed that we should fight save with thyself alone, and it is harder for us to contend with yonder animal than with thee." And Owain put the lion in the place where the maiden had been imprisoned, and blocked up the door with stones, and he went to fight with the young men, as before. But Owain had not his usual strength, and the two youths pressed hard upon him. And the lion roared incessantly at seeing Owain in trouble; and he burst through the wall until he found a way out, and rushed upon the young men, and instantly slew them. So Luned was saved from being burned.

Then Owain returned with Luned to the dominions of the Countess of the Fountain. And when he went thence he took the Countess with him to Arthur's Court, and she was his wife as long as she lived.

And then he took the road that led to the Court of the savage black man, and Owain fought with him, and the lion did not quit Owain until he had vanquished him. And when he reached the Court of the savage black man he entered the hall, and beheld four-and-twenty ladies, the fairest that could be seen. And the garments which they had on were not worth four-and twenty pence, and they were as sorrowful as death. And Owain asked them the cause of their sadness. And they said, "We are the daughters of Earls, and we all came here with our husbands, whom we dearly loved. And we were received with honour and rejoicing. And we were thrown into a state of stupor, and while we were thus, the demon who owns this Castle slew all our husbands, and took from us our horses, and our raiment, and our gold, and our silver; and the corpses of our husbands are still in this house, and many others with them. And this, Chieftain, is the cause of our grief, and we are sorry that thou art come hither, lest harm should befall thee."

And Owain was grieved when he heard this. And he went forth from the Castle, and he beheld a knight approaching him, who saluted him in a friendly and cheerful manner, as if he had been a brother. And this was the savage black man. "In very sooth," said Owain, "it is not to seek thy friendship that I am here." "In sooth," said he, "thou shalt not find it then." And with that they charged each other, and fought furiously. And Owain overcame him, and bound his hands behind his back. Then the black savage besought Owain to spare his life, and spoke thus: "My lord Owain," said he, "it was foretold that thou shouldst come hither and vanquish me, and thou hast done so. I was a robber here, and my house was a house of spoil; but grant me my life, and I will become the keeper of an Hospice, and I will maintain this house as an

Hospice for weak and for strong, as long as I live, for the good of thy soul." And Owain accepted this proposal of him, and remained there that night.

And the next day he took the four-and-twenty ladies, and their horses, and their raiment, and what they possessed of goods and jewels, and proceeded with them to Arthur's Court. And if Arthur was rejoiced when he saw him, after he had lost him the first time, his joy was now much greater. And of those ladies, such as wished to remain in Arthur's Court remained there, and such as wished to depart departed.

And thenceforward Owain dwelt at Arthur's Court greatly beloved, as the head of his household, until he went away with his followers; and those were the army of three hundred ravens which Kenverchyn had left him. And wherever Owain went with these he was victorious.

And this is the tale of THE LADY OF THE FOUNTAIN.

Arthurian Songs: 1. Avalon

Rachel Annand Taylor (1894)

King Arthur lies alone
Deep down in Avalon.
Alone! For what fair knight
Is loyal quite?
Could golden Pelleas be lain
To drowse between delight and pain?
Could Tristram's musique here be borne,
Or the great blast of Gawain's horn?
It is no land for Galahad
Where none are good and none are bad.
It is no land for Lancelot
Where sweet and bitter are forgot.
For that proud soul of Guenevere's,
And her long ransom of bright tears
It is no land,—where none may weep,
Between reveillé and faint sleep.
Swung soft 'tween heaven and hell, it seems
A crystal in a cloud of dreams.
Yet doth some one pass that way.
Is it, is it Morgan la Faye?—
Saying: "Was it love or hate?"
Saying: "But the wound is great."
So, amid the poppies white,
Long rests Arthur, King and Knight.
King Arthur lies alone,
Deep down in Avalon.
Alone! For what fair knight
Is loyal quite?

Sir Galahad, a Christmas Mystery

William Morris (1858)

It is the longest night in all the year,
Near on the day when
the Lord Christ was born;
Six hours ago I came and sat down here,
And ponder'd sadly, wearied and forlorn.

The winter wind that pass'd
the chapel door,
Sang out a moody tune,
that went right well
With mine own thoughts:
I look'd down on the floor,
Between my feet, until I heard a bell

Sound a long way off
through the forest deep,
And toll on steadily; a drowsiness
Came on me, so that I fell half asleep,
As I sat there not moving: less and less

I saw the melted snow that hung in beads
Upon my steel-shoes; less and less I saw
Between the tiles the
bunches of small weeds:
Heartless and stupid, with no touch of awe

Upon me, half-shut eyes upon the ground,
I thought: O Galahad! the days go by,
Stop and cast up now that
which you have found,
So sorely you have wrought and painfully.

Night after night your
horse treads down alone
The sere damp fern,
night after night you sit
Holding the bridle like a man of stone,
Dismal, unfriended:
what thing comes of it?

And what if Palomydes also ride,
And over many a
mountain and bare heath
Follow the questing beast
with none beside?
Is he not able still to hold his breath

With thoughts of Iseult?
doth he not grow pale
With weary striving, to seem best of all
To her, "as she is best," he saith? to fail
Is nothing to him, he can never fall.

For unto such a man love-sorrow is
So dear a thing unto his constant heart,
That even if he never win one kiss,
Or touch from Iseult, it will never part.

And he will never know her to be worse
Than in his happiest dreams
he thinks she is:
Good knight, and faithful,
you have 'scaped the curse
In wonderful-wise;
you have great store of bliss.

Sir Gawain and the Green Knight, The Lady of Shallot, The Lady of the Fountain, and other Classic Poems and Tales of Camelot

Yea, what if Father Launcelot ride out,
Can he not think of
Guenevere's arms, round
Warm and lithe, about his neck, and shout
Till all the place grows
joyful with the sound?

And when he lists can often see her face,
And think, "Next month I kiss you,
or next week,
And still you think of me":
therefore the place
Grows very pleasant, whatsoever he seek.

But me, who ride alone,
some carle shall find
Dead in my arms in the half-melted snow,
When all unkindly with the shifting wind,
The thaw comes on at Candlemas: I know

Indeed that they will say: "This Galahad
If he had lived had been
a right good knight;
Ah! poor chaste body!"
but they will be glad,
Not most alone, but all, when in their sight

That very evening in their scarlet sleeves
The gay-dress'd minstrels sing;
no maid will talk
Of sitting on my tomb, until the leaves,
Grown big upon the bushes of the walk,

East of the Palace-pleasaunce,
make it hard
To see the minster therefrom: well-a-day!

Before the trees by autumn
were well bared,
I saw a damozel with gentle play,

Within that very walk say last farewell
To her dear knight, just riding out to find
(Why should I choke to say it?)
the Sangreal,
And their last kisses sunk into my mind,

Yea, for she stood lean'd
forward on his breast,
Rather, scarce stood;
the back of one dear hand,
That it might well be kiss'd,
she held and press'd
Against his lips;
long time they stood there, fann'd

By gentle gusts of quiet frosty wind,
Till Mador de la porte a-going by,
And my own horsehoofs roused them;
they untwined,
And parted like a dream. In this way I,

With sleepy face bent to the chapel floor,
Kept musing half asleep, till suddenly
A sharp bell rang from
close beside the door,
And I leapt up when
something pass'd me by,

Shrill ringing going with it, still half blind
I stagger'd after, a great sense of awe
At every step kept gathering on my mind,
Thereat I have no marvel, for I saw

85

Sir Gawain and the Green Knight, The Lady of Shallot, The Lady of the Fountain, and other Classic Poems and Tales of Camelot

One sitting on the altar as a throne,
Whose face no man could
say he did not know,
And though the bell still rang, he sat alone,
With raiment half blood-red, half white as
snow.

Right so I fell upon the floor and knelt,
Not as one kneels in church
when mass is said,
But in a heap, quite nerveless, for I felt
The first time what a thing
was perfect dread.

But mightily the gentle voice came down:
"Rise up, and look and listen, Galahad,
Good knight of God,
for you will see no frown
Upon my face; I come to make you glad.

"For that you say that you are all alone,
I will be with you always, and fear not
You are uncared for,
though no maiden moan
Above your empty tomb; for Launcelot,

"He in good time shall be my servant too,
Meantime, take note whose sword first
made him knight,
And who has loved him
alway, yea, and who
Still trusts him alway,
though in all men's sight,

"He is just what you know, O Galahad,
This love is happy even as you say,
But would you for a little time be glad,
To make ME sorry long, day after day?

"Her warm arms round
his neck half throttle ME,
The hot love-tears burn
deep like spots of lead,
Yea, and the years pass quick:
right dismally
Will Launcelot at one time hang his head;

"Yea, old and shrivell'd
he shall win my love.
Poor Palomydes fretting out his soul!
Not always is he able, son, to move
His love, and do it honour:
needs must roll

"The proudest destrier
sometimes in the dust,
And then 'tis weary work;
he strives beside
Seem better than he is, so that his trust
Is always on what chances may betide;

"And so he wears away, my servant, too,
When all these things are gone,
and wretchedly
He sits and longs to moan for Iseult, who
Is no care now to Palomydes: see,

"O good son, Galahad, upon this day,
Now even, all these things
are on your side,
But these you fight not for; look up, I say,
And see how I can love you, for no pride

"Closes your eyes, no vain
lust keeps them down.
See now you have ME always; following
That holy vision, Galahad, go on,
Until at last you come to ME to sing

Sir Gawain and the Green Knight, The Lady of Shallot, The Lady of the Fountain,
and other Classic Poems and Tales of Camelot

"In Heaven always, and to walk around
  The garden where I am."
    He ceased, my face
And wretched body fell upon the ground;
And when I look'd again, the holy place

Was empty; but right so the bell again
Came to the chapel-door, there entered
Two angels first, in white, without a stain,
And scarlet wings, then, after them, a bed

Four ladies bore, and set it down beneath
  The very altar-step, and while for fear
    I scarcely dared to move
      or draw my breath,
Those holy ladies gently came a-near,

And quite unarm'd me, saying: "Galahad,
    Rest here awhile and sleep,
      and take no thought
Of any other thing than being glad;
    Hither the Sangreal will
      be shortly brought,

"Yet must you sleep the
  while it stayeth here."
Right so they went away, and I,
      being weary,
Slept long and dream'd of Heaven:
    the bell comes near,
I doubt it grows to morning. Miserere!

Enter Two Angels in white, with scarlet
wings; also, Four Ladies in gowns of red
and green; also an Angel, bearing in his
hands a surcoat of white, with a red cross.

AN ANGEL

O servant of the high God, Galahad!
    Rise and be arm'd:
  the Sangreal is gone forth
    Through the great forest,
      and you must be had
Unto the sea that lieth on the north:

    There shall you find
    the wondrous ship wherein
The spindles of King Solomon are laid,
    And the sword that no man
      draweth without sin,
But if he be most pure: and there is stay'd,

    Hard by, Sir Launcelot,
      whom you will meet
In some short space upon that ship:
      first, though,
Will come here presently that lady sweet,
Sister of Percival, whom you well know,

  And with her Bors and Percival:
      stand now,
  These ladies will to arm you.

FIRST LADY, putting on the hauberk
      Galahad,
    That I may stand so close
      beneath your brow,
  Margaret of Antioch, am glad.

    SECOND LADY,
    girding him with the sword.
    That I may stand and
      touch you with my hand,
O Galahad, I, Cecily, am glad.

THIRD LADY, buckling on the spurs.
That I may kneel while
up above you stand,
And gaze at me, O holy Galahad,
I, Lucy, am most glad.

FOURTH LADY, putting on the basnet.
O gentle knight,
That you bow down to us in reverence,
We are most glad, I,
Katherine, with delight
Must needs fall trembling.

ANGEL, putting on the crossed surcoat.
Galahad, we go hence,
For here, amid the straying of the snow,
Come Percival's sister, Bors, and Percival.
The Four Ladies carry out the bed,
and all go but Galahad.

GALAHAD

How still and quiet everything seems now:
They come, too,
for I hear the horsehoofs fall.

Enter Sir Bors, Sir Percival and his Sister.

Fair friends and gentle lady,
God you save!
A many marvels have been here to-night;
Tell me what news of
Launcelot you have,
And has God's body ever been in sight?

SIR BORS

Why, as for seeing that same holy thing,
As we were riding slowly side by side,
An hour ago, we heard a sweet voice sing,
And through the bare twigs saw a great
light glide,

With many-colour'd raiment, but far off;
And so pass'd quickly:
from the court nought good;
Poor merry Dinadan,
that with jape and scoff
Kept us all merry, in a little wood

Was found all hack'd and dead: Sir Lionel
And Gauwaine have come
back from the great quest,
Just merely shamed; and Lauvaine,
who loved well
Your father Launcelot,
at the king's behest

Went out to seek him,
but was almost slain,
Perhaps is dead now; everywhere
The knights come foil'd
from the great quest, in vain;
In vain they struggle for the vision fair.